The Oppressors

by

Samira Al-Mana

Translated from Arabic

by Paul Starkey

and the author

Samira al-Mana is an Iraqi fiction writer. She was born and grew up in Basra, Iraq and now lives in London. Her publications include six novels, two collections of short stories and a play. From 1985 to 2002 she was assistant editor of the Arabic Magazine ALIGHTIRAB AL-ADABI (Literature of the Exiled); www.alightirab.cjb.net

Some of her short stories have been translated into English and published in various magazines and fiction anthologies of the Middle East. Her novel (The Umbilical Cord) was translated and published in 2005.

Published in 2011 by YouWriteOn.com

Copyright © Text Samira Al-Mana

First Edition

The author asserts the moral right under the Copyright, Designs and Patents Act 1988 to be identified as the author of this work.

All Rights reserved. No part of this publication may be reproduced, stored in a retrieval system, or transmitted, in any form or by any means without the prior written consent of the author, nor be otherwise circulated in any form of binding or cover other than that in which it is published and without a similar condition being imposed on the subsequent purchaser.

Published by YouWriteOn.com

Acknowledgements

It is through funding from the Arts Council England and with the help of the Exiled Writers Ink organisation that an extract from this novella was translated and published first as a chapbook.

My gratitude goes to Jennifer Langer and Nathalie Teitler from Exiled Writers Ink, together with the Arts Council England, for their assistance by instigating the scheme of translation of exiled writers' work into English and bringing it to public attention.

I owe thanks also to Professor Paul Starkey who took the initiative in translating the first chapter of the novella, which encouraged me to translate the whole book later.

None of this would have happened if I did not have the support of my husband Salah Niazi, who shares my belief that literature is the very essence of our daily life.

The book has been edited and prepared for publication by Ghislaine Stevenson. My daughter, Sara Niazi, designed the cover to reflect the theme of the story – I thank both of them with all my heart.

Introduction

'The Oppressors' was originally written in 1968. A long period has passed between writing and its printing in Arabic in 1997 – nearly 29 years. During this period many books appeared on Iraq, including three novels of mine. These focused mainly on the dominant political issues, starting with the terrible war between Iraq and Iran which flared up in 1980 and dragged on for eight years. Then followed the invasion of Kuwait in 1990 and finally the UN sanctions, which lasted twelve years. During this period an enormously high number of deaths among Iraqi children were recorded. In addition large numbers of people fled the country.

The 'Oppressors' does not deal with these key issues as it was written in 1968. It deals instead with the ordinary people of Iraq, and what happens when the oppressed change their status.

It becomes clear that the outcome is not as positive as might be hoped. Indeed, the victims become victimisers, oppressing others and inflicting perhaps even more suffering than they themselves suffered.

Chapter One

One Baghdad winter's night – a night so dark that the sky seemed to merge into the earth – a great commotion could be heard coming from a room in the Faculty of Languages girls' hostel. Miss Mary, the hostel Principal, hurried out in alarm, preparing herself to punish the girls who were fooling around in such an annoying way. As it turned out, though, the punishment was forgotten in her alarm, and the girls were preserved from any imminent danger. Miss Mary had been about to go to bed, taking out the clips from her grey, lifeless hair so that it stood on end, totally dishevelled. She pushed at the half-open door of their room quickly, like someone lifting up a blazing cauldron from the fire, and eight iron bedsteads appeared spread out over the length and breadth of the room. The girls leaped around her in groups, pleading for help, some half dressed, others in their nightdresses, and some still in their day clothes. She scolded them in an agitated way, nothing deflecting her from her attack. The fact that they were disturbed, scared and frightened was no bar to her sternness – though for the moment, she contented herself with a good telling-off, saving their punishment until later.

'Have you gone mad? Are you in your right minds?'

A girl gestured with her hand at the window overlooking the garden, like a dumb person, unable to speak. She was followed by another girl, then by the others, one after another like the beads of a necklace, eager that it should not be broken.

They began to speak, fearfully and hesitantly: 'Miss Mary, Miss Mary! Thieves were watching from outside the window!'

She shook them from her shoulders with a quite unscrupulous and unfeeling roughness.

'Thieves? What is this? Impossible!'

Once again they crowded around her, pleading, and desperately trying to convince her. One girl boldly took the lead: 'Believe us, Miss Mary, we saw them. Their faces were up against that window!'

The girl gestured again with her finger. It was an accusation. But Miss Mary was determined to make light of it. She brushed aside their fears. 'Be quiet, that's enough! Don't be so silly!'

Her rebuke didn't do any good. They were sticking together. One of them began to measure out her words with that fine heavenly balance that she always possessed while defending herself:

'Miss Mary, I swear by the soul of my father. I saw their faces from the window with my own eyes!'

Another backed up what she had said even more boldly:

'Yes, by God, that's right!'

Miss Mary stood in the middle of them, rocking slightly in her loose fitting nightclothes. She was decidedly on the plump side, and her body was flabby and bloated. She had come straight out of her room, but reluctantly – she wouldn't have done if it hadn't been for the girls. Meanwhile, the caretaker Jasim had hurriedly grabbed the hem of his *dishdasha* and emerged from his room, his face long with fear as he imagined a fire had broken out in the building. He came into the room without asking permission, shaking so hard with fear that if he had had a candle in his hand it would have certainly gone out.

'What's going on, what's going on?'

Miss Mary folded her arms. She found it an ideal opportunity to tell him off and to warn him to be more careful about preserving security.

'Don't pretend to be ignorant! Do you really not know that burglars have got into the garden and been spying on the girls from the windows?'

Jasim said nothing, then prepared to defend himself putting forward arguments – feeble ones in Miss Mary's eyes – in the hope that she would not be too harsh. He knew well she wasn't always exactly kind and forgiving, so he began swearing the most sacred oaths. 'By my honour, Miss Mary, I was awake in my room!'

'And what were you doing, may I ask? Were you listening to the radio?'

He swallowed hard. She was making fun of him, disbelieving what he said. He pulled himself together again. He was swimming with the tide in order to avoid drowning in the deeper waters.

'Sometimes, but I'm always listening out on the girls' behalf. I'm always with the girls, even when I'm listening to the radio!'

Miss Mary's expression suddenly changed as she adopted a new strategy. She was standing there holding him to account, in a position of authority, face to face, using a powerful inquisitorial technique as if she were one of the students who were complaining.

'Didn't you hear or see these people who came into the garden?'

'No, I swear!'

'The girls swear that they saw them!'

A particularly daring girl emerged from the crowd, completely free of embarrassment. 'I saw them with my own eyes, I swear I did.'

Jasim was at a loss. 'Where did they come from? The outside gate is shut and my room is opposite the entrance from the garden.'

The girl argued with him gently but firmly, a little nervously.

It was obvious that the argument could have gone on, but Miss Mary ended it with a decisive teacher's blow: 'Jasim is responsible for security, that's the beginning and the end of it. Whether they came through the main door or across the fence. The important thing is, this is an obvious complaint against you as an employee, which I'll be submitting tomorrow to the university administration.'

Jasim was stunned. He was holding on to what remained of his self-control. He was used to her sometimes making threats, then being placated.

'God forgive you, Miss Mary. You believe the girls and you don't believe me!'

Miss Mary bit her lip.

'I believe the persons who saw it with their own eyes,' she said suddenly, in a tone of anger and contempt.

The final blow had brought with it an even more ferocious attack. She left the room, her mind made up. Jasim remained there, not knowing what to do, then crept out with a worried look, his quivering eyebrows only making things worse. He searched the garden here and there. His frame could be spotted between the trees and the paths, and the back walls of the girls' hostel. It didn't last long. Emergency police cars arrived, summoned by telephone by Miss Mary. Boots, leather belts, the clank of iron and the glint of brass followed one another in quick succession. They searched inside and out, out of breath, making threats and discovering nothing. Just as the caretaker Jasim had discovered nothing. The results of the investigations were collected and preserved in files registered with a number and a title.

* * * * *

The following day, the Dean of the College of Languages did his duty. He contacted the Public Security Directorate, emphasising the need to guard the hostel without a break, stressing the importance of a police presence in front of the gate for security at the present time. The girls are under our protection. They should have proper security. At the same time, this extraordinary incident somehow found a voice and a brightness of its own. It matured on the chairs of the Faculty of Languages messengers, and was picked up by the infatuated male students, who made fun of the girls, and saw it as a piece of out-of-the-ordinary fantasy. They imagined the thieves to be daring folk. They infringed upon the strained hostel and intruded on what was going on inside the rooms of their female colleagues. They described with relish the girls' clothes and their beds in fine detail that included more than ordinary thieves would be concerned with. The Dean and the revered professors were just as bad. They exchanged smiles as soon as they heard the news. They repeatedly touched on the subject, wondering what the thieves could be wanting in the girls' hostel, and alluding obscurely but jokingly to their feminine condition.

The Faculty of Languages girls' hostel is situated on the main road, with a piece of wasteland behind it. It was rumoured that the owner had intended to build a block of flats on it, but the building was never put up and the rear windows of the hostel continued to look out at a wide empty space which stretched between two streets, leading the eye to the Faculty of Languages men's hostel. The male students were forced to go along the main street and to pass the girls' building with its polished oak door, which was seldom without the caretaker Jasim sitting by it, on his chair with the flowery cotton seat. He was the only man who was officially permitted to enter the building whenever he wished. He was the girls' defender, from everything imaginable and unimaginable alike. He also had the authority to talk to the girls as they came in and went out. He could bid them good morning and good evening and return their greetings. He addressed Miss Mary in a way that could almost have indicated a close family relationship, had it not been mingled with a touch of fear and hypocrisy as well. His good manners prevented him from going into their rooms without asking permission. The way they looked caused the caretaker Jasim to find that it infringed his sense of decency – sometimes they were sleeping, sometimes undressing, and sometimes laughing. When they asked him to buy them something, drinks or notebooks, for example, he would obey their demands with dignity and respect, knocking on the room door and muttering to alert anyone that cared that Jasim had arrived.

These rooms were a monotonously ordered chain. Each of them contained iron beds and wooden cupboards resting against the walls, the same colour and size. They were separated from each other by small wooden side tables large enough for no more than a book and a few pens. The girls used them as make-up tables and sometimes put fruit and a glass of water on them.

* * * * *

Hasan the policemen smiled, like a snake charmer getting ready, preening himself, eager that his stories should please Jasim. The latter's job did not hold any importance or flavour for him. It wasn't a real job in Hasan's eyes; it was idleness in another guise, compared to his.

'Yes, Jasim, we were chasing them, a black Chevrolet car. We went after it at full speed. We'd left the border behind, gone further than the Safwan post. We were in the desert in no-man's-land. Officer Majid said 'Shoot!', and the bullets burst. Your friend, Hasan, aimed at it with a nice bullet that punctured one of its tyres. The wheel-rims hit the ground and stopped. It was smuggled goods this time, from Kuwait to Basra. Bah, bah, bah!'

'You were in Basra at the time?' Jasim interrupted in a surprised tone to please the bragging policeman. But the policeman corrected him: 'No, no, not just in Basra but the whole of the southern Iraqi border. Iran, Kuwait, Saudi, I was everywhere, you name it. That year we caught five hundred smugglers' vehicles.'

With this last expression the policeman scared the caretaker Jasim. He roared with laughter, and he looked as though his hand was about to box Jasim's ears.

'Exactly.'

'I was in Basra three years, Y*a, ya, ya* and two in Nasiriyya, *ya, ya, ya.* And now here I am in Baghdad, *wai, wai, wai.* Where did we get to in the story, sir?'

'To the smuggling.'

'No, no, no, you don't know anything. I don't just mean smuggling. There are other important things that happened there.

'Go on.'

'This is an old story that happened eight years ago. But it's an important story, quite well known. The people involved are also well known and the witnesses are still alive. I was in Amara at the time. It was a girl of a good family. One night the devil got into her and she ran away from home. Not a trace of her, not a clue where she was. I won't drag the story out; the police and her family were looking for her but to no avail. Inspector Raghib summoned me and said to me: 'Hasan, you're a wonder at these things. You're on the ball. Get out on the case at once.' Blimey. So I went out on the case. For three days I looked for her. I left no stone unturned. On the third day, I caught her. I found her with her lover heading by boat across the Shatt al-Arab waterway towards Abadan in Iran. She said: 'He's my husband, I married him in front of witnesses!' But what's the use of words or deeds? The important thing is, I restored respect to her family and took a payment from her brother. May God reward him well! He was a true son of his father. By God, yes! He plunged the knife straight into her heart. No questions, no answers. In front of the police station. And why not? He bore no responsibility. A killing to restore the family's honour. He wasn't to blame. No more than a sentence of two years in jail.'

'The Devil, these bitches follow the Devil!' muttered Jasim, opening an old wound. He adjusted the skullcap on his head, careful not to say anything else to the policeman who had taken up his position at the entrance to the girls' dormitory three days ago. He had brought his things, which amounted to no more than a camp bed, with a tin trunk to hold his possessions and a folding chair. In the corner stood a long-necked water jar. He was wanting to finish his story, but a girl peeped out through a crack in the door, asking 'Uncle' Jasim to bring her four bottles of juice. He obliged, taking off his sandals as though he wanted to run, he was so eager. Then he put them on again as he always did when he wanted to get up, adjusting his chair, with ninety *fils* sticking to his palm. 'Is that all you have left? Is this the sum total of what you are guarding at this moment, Jasim?' But the officer Hasan didn't want him to get up. He was insisting on finishing his tales and adventures.

'I'll have to interrupt the conversation', Jasim said.

'Don't be long.'

'I'll take my own time.'

The phrase escaped from Jasim's mouth without his being conscious of it. He wasn't very happy with it.

'No, no, come on!' said the policeman, warning and urging him at the same time. Jasim shrunk away from him, leaving the doorway under protest. He no longer had anything except children's work: 'Come here, go there!' Work that shouldn't be undertaken by someone who just a week ago had made men and women afraid! The policeman was occupying his territory, his revolver at his hip, sitting in the middle of the doorway like a sultan. Jasim came back after a little while, dragging his feet, and the policeman greeted him cheerily: 'Ha, you've come back!'

'What do you think!' replied Jasim sarcastically. He was annoyed, brimming with anger in fact, and quivering. 'Do you want me not to come then?' He felt that Hasan would definitely be double-crossing him and taking his place, moving him out, in fact yes, definitely. The policeman was a rival who needed to be taken care of. The water would flow under him and his job would disappear. It was just like when his wife Naema had left him several years ago, when a taxi driver had become his rival for her affection. Then, when Jasim returned to the village which he left three years before, he did not find her with his family. Bitches, they follow the Devil, and are afraid of thieves! He gritted his teeth.

'Are you going to sleep? Come on, come on! The night is still young!' called the policeman in his enticing way.

'No,' replied Jasim curtly, finishing the conversation. 'I'm really tired.' And he went off to his room, having given the girl the bottles of juice.

His room was at the entrance to the building. It had a small window facing the main road. There was also another window looking over the entrance that 'Uncle' Jasim regarded as a third eye in his head. Through this he could control who went into or out of the building. Through the outer window he could even observe the intentions of people looking at the building. Jasim went into his room and shut the door in protest, but he still found Naema and the policeman and the driver crouching there. He sat down on the bed, cursing the Devil. A cold wind was meanwhile blowing through the window, and little by little sounds of singing began to drift in from outside. The sounds were lost in the broad street, but then crept insistently inside, to every corner of the house – the lively voices of the male students returning from their amusements at the end of the evening, intoxicated as they passed under the walls of the locked, forbidden hostel. Songs burst forth from their throats. Naema had liked singing. Their neighbour Zaynab had told him that while he was away she used to go out with the driver of the red taxi, in which the sound of singing could often be heard on the radio. The voices got closer to the building, there was more singing, the students' feet like a broom knocking against the walls. There were lots of voices, like an onslaught of sound:

> 'If you complain of passion,
> you are not one of us,
> apple of my eye, my love.
> Bear cruelty and rejection,
> apple of my eye, my love ...'

What eye could not see it? Jasim folded his legs beneath himself and bravely remembered. The song was his guide and his light. He realised who the intruders were that memorable night, when some people had thought burglars had got into the building. Now he had managed to solve the theft, something that no one else had been able to discover, not even the Dean or his assistant or policeman Hasan. Jasim alone knew the secret. He wished he could stop these drunken revellers and send them to the police station at once. He would drag them by their collars, making fun of them and exposing their secrets so that the girls would laugh at them, while policeman Hasan was fast asleep. What was he to do with these thieves? One group was guffawing and another singing boisterously. Jasim swallowed hard, eaten up by anger, as he realised that the girls had been deluded into believing that they were thieves who had crept in that night, looking through the window to strike terror into the building. They were just lunatics, making a mockery of the law and our customs. Perhaps to make a date or get a sight of a girl inside. A girl like Naema with her round face and delicate eyebrows. His arms shook as he saw them approaching the window, which had almost started to quake. He wished he could start a fight with cudgels and spitting. To wake up the girls' stupid fathers and punish the policeman who had gone to sleep. Except that he smelt the scent of the plump Naema, warming the bed of the driver of the red taxi and speaking with difficulty, while the song in the street went off at a tangent, slowly moving away from him, heading for the male students' dormitory that was situated about half a mile away. The voices disappeared, leaving not a single trace behind. The room turned cold, enfolding the caretaker Jasim who had fallen silent as a deep dark well, unable to speak.

* * * * *

The girls' hostel sign that hung above the door enjoyed special attention. Once a month it was lifted off its nails and the dust removed. Jasim the caretaker was experienced enough to know how to bring out the colour of the wood so that it would not fade. He would sometimes polish it with varnish, using a rag to make the colour shine, to highlight the white letters inscribed on it that announced the girls' hostel to whoever saw it.

He craned his neck back and stood on tiptoe as he forced the plaque back into place. When he had finished, the policeman shouted at him with some advice: 'The left side is crooked!'

Jasim was reluctant to believe him, tilting the sign to the right, as he measured it in his special, tortuous way, making sure that the letters were straight. There was no longer a problem with the sides. He shook the piece of cloth on the wall as he got ready to wipe the door as well, polishing the nails, the yellow buttons and the knocker to make it seem shinier and more impressive. He would have liked to rub up and down its sides in a spiral pattern, taking out a protrusion here and hiding a splinter of wood there. He polished it again and again with the policeman stretched out near him, with his pillow folded, missing nothing that was going on around him. There was a lot going on, for as well as Jasim and his futile exertions, girls were coming in and going out. The girl with the plaits came back and another one left. Good Lord, how many were coming and going that day! He laughed to himself, dredging up a dirty joke from his memory. He hoped that Jasim who was busy with the building sign would like it. Who should he talk to, if his friend was busy with the door, as if it was the sacred gate of the al-Kadhim shrine?

'Jasim, come on, come here!' He called him, straining all the muscles in his neck, as if to say 'What's come over you' in an intimidating way.

'I'm busy, my friend', replied Jasim sternly, telling him off, his anger aroused.

The policeman hunched himself up again, disappointed, and stretched out his hand angrily to take his tin of tobacco. He smoked a cigarette before sitting down carefully. From under his bed he took out a metal cup, soap and a brush. He got up from his place to ladle some water from the bucket with the cup. Finally, he sat down, tilting his face as he washed the dust from his beard, spitting out soap and water beside him. Then he went back to his bed, tossing and turning from left to right. Jasim the caretaker was still busy with his polishing. Hasan knew that the man was engrossed. There was no point in pressing him. He sat himself up again to drink some water from the jar; then went back to his pillow. He glared at everyone who strutted in front of him. One girl attracted his attention. Why had she gone out so much this morning? Was there a fox of some sort lurking somewhere? What harm would it do to ask Jasim why a girl like her should be coming in and going out more than twice in one morning? He struck his hands together with a sigh before he picked up the sound of Jasim's chair scraping at the door. His features lit up and he returned to his normal position. So Jasim had finished at last! Every folly has an end, he thought to himself. His quiver was full of all sorts of subjects and comments which he desperately wanted to direct at Jasim at any cost. 'Jasim, have you finished?' he called to him politely.

'Ha!'

'Do you know what I mean?' asked the policeman, guffawing with laughter and trying to lead him on.

'No!'

'Come here, then, come on!'

The words crowded together in his throat, almost spilling out. Jasim attached no importance to that: 'What do you want from me, my friend?'

'I've got a problem', joked the officer, trying to appear friendly. But Jasim was insistent on his principles: 'Leave it for now, another time!' he said.

'No, it's urgent. Come on, please!'

'Who is this idiot? What does this braggart want from me?' Jasim adjusted his skullcap and tied his shoelaces, checking that they were firmly in place. Yes, the shoes. Indeed the day of wearing shoes had arrived. Whenever he wanted to impress his superiors he would put aside his everyday sandals. Perhaps an official would come today to view the building, after the imagined attempted theft, and then they would see Jasim and give him his due. Someone had to take notice of him. What was the policeman's pride in his wrinkled, dusty shoes compared with Jasim's shining new shoes that never saw the light of day except on high days and holidays? He wiped his brow, remembering his important role. The great occasion had now arrived in which friend could be distinguished from foe and he could scent the smell of authority, even if it was in the shoes. The policeman rolled over on his bed shouting with excitement. His patience was exhausted. 'OK, I'll come to you!'

Jasim, full of pride, despised him. 'Come on, then!'

The policeman pulled the bottom of his bench closer. It was like his chair, only used occasionally, since the bed was opposite it. He rolled up his sleeves, tapping Jasim on the shoulder, and winking at him gently: 'Excellent, a real chick, excellent!'

Jasim couldn't forgive him. Hasan was pointing at a passing girl. He hated him intensely at that moment. It was only Mayada, from Basra. She had brought him a box of dates as a present after visiting her family there. One day she had asked him to buy her a notebook and had given him the change from a dinar. It was the end of the month and had come at the right time. Jasim looked at his shoes and the policeman went back to his game. 'That one', he said, like someone giving away a secret. 'She went out, then came back, went out and came back. Were you watching her? Did you see her? I don't know what's come over her, really I don't.'

'Who?'

'That one, that one, there she is, coming back. Look, look at her, she's coming now.'

Nahla appeared at last through the gate leading to the garden. She opened it to come in, calm and full of poise. She greeted 'Uncle' Jasim as usual. The policeman smoothed aside his bushy moustache to join in, returning her greeting. Silence returned for a little while. Then at midday crowds of girls arrived from outside, happy and merry, creating more problems for 'Uncle' Jasim as they gave the policeman their full attention. Jasim was so shaken that he got up angrily from where he was sitting.

'Where are you going?' asked the policeman in surprise.

'I've got work to do inside.'

'Now?'

'Yes.'

'I've hardly seen you today.'

'Thank God!'

He cut an arrogant pose as he left the place to go into the hall of the girls' hostel. Someone was on the telephone, and he could see Nahla's head. He slipped behind her, trying to get away quickly, desperately trying to control himself. How he would have liked to have seized the policeman by the neck, and pursue the quarrel to court, were it not for his restraint. What was Nahla up to and who was she speaking to?

He walked away from her a little. He heard her speaking to someone. The sound of his shoes striking the ground made him feel that he really existed. Nahla resumed her conversation. Her head moved in his direction. Who did Nahla have in Baghdad? Could it be her brother? Or her cousin, or someone else.... It annoyed him to think that Nahla should be speaking to someone he didn't know, as if she was actually ignoring him. He felt bitter and preoccupied; the policeman was like a second wife, competing with him for his position, wanting to be treated in the same way. He was watching the girls whenever he wanted, sometimes smiling with them, returning their greetings morning and evening. Jasim was angry and annoyed as he came back to him with a heavy heart. The policeman saw him from a distance and leapt up from the chair reserved for Jasim alone beside the door. No one except him had dared to sit on his chair with the flowery cotton seat before. For the rest, the policeman behaved politely. 'Jasim, your seat. Take your place!' he said, getting up from the seat to make way for him.

Jasim responded hesitantly, turning his face away from him, for fear that his hypocrisy might be seen openly. 'No, no, stay where you are, so long as you are comfortable.'

'How? And you? Where will you sit?'

'Here, I'll sit there.'

He pointed to the policeman's narrow bench that he had brought with his things and which was not even wide enough for a handkerchief. He folded his arms around his knees, to protect himself from anything that might happen. The policeman's face lit up. He imagined himself saying: 'What do you think now, sir, who's more deserving of sitting on this comfortable chair, me with my trousers and revolver at my side, or you with your *dishdasha* and stupid skullcap?'

Jasim swallowed the humiliation. Let Abla walk in on them and the policeman return her greeting, then! There was nothing left except to cut this man's throat. How could he dare greet her? Who had given him the idea of taking his chair? All it needed now was for him to go into the building whenever he liked and stand at the door of Abla's room – or Salma's, or Siham's. What was there to protect them from his wicked eyes which followed them and challenged Jasim? His suspicions gnawed away at him. He got up like a man distraught.

'Where are you going? Why are you getting up?' asked the policeman.

'For lunch', replied Jasim curtly. His pain was obvious as he approached Miss Mary's room, intending to bring her food as usual, knocking on the door.

'Who is it? Sadea?' enquired the woman from inside the room.

'No it's me, Jasim, I'll bring lunch.'

'And where's Sadea?'

'I don't know. I'll bring your lunch anyway.'

'Okay. Call Sadea on your way!'

He did what Miss Mary wanted and added something of his own, to avenge himself on anyone who was not afraid of him and had no business in the building. He was in a hurry. The food was waiting for him in the cafeteria and he also had things to do. They couldn't be compared with Sadea the cleaner's duties. What was the point of sweeping the floor as far as he was concerned? Why was it so important to clean the washbasins and baths? The day was long and Sadea had enough time to do all these stupid things. What had come over this lazy Sadea? She could spin out a day's work for a year. Sadea was in the kitchen eating broth. She was startled by his sudden, angry appearance. He told her off sharply as if she was an idiot.

'Where have you been?'

'Why? What's happened?'

She quickly threw the broth away, groping for her words carefully like a blind woman.

'Are you deaf?' We've been shouting for you a thousand times, with no reply!'

'Jasim, by the honour of the prophet, I didn't hear anything.'

'The Queen wants you!'

Sadea seemed even more stupid than usual. She repeated the expression, then thought a bit and finally realised who he meant by the 'Queen'. 'Miss Mary wants me?'

'No, she wants the blind and the deaf!' said Jasim, flying into a rage as he left the room, leaving Sadea terrified. The broth still glistened on her lips and fingers, as well as in the bowl.

* * * * *

The distance between the girls' hostel and the Faculty cafeteria was a real journey by Jasim's scale of reckoning. He would wave his hand in salute to the laundry man, Salman, and bellow another greeting to Master Rajab, who owned the domestic appliance shop, if he was standing at the door. Sometimes he would dawdle near him, to exchange a brief chat. He wouldn't want to stay long, especially as someone would no doubt be waiting for him, perhaps a student, perhaps Miss Mary, or perhaps he would just be sitting on his chair to guard the building. He could find excuses for delaying, if he wanted to, for the cafeteria was always late and the food wasn't ready, and had it not been for his persistence with the chef Miss Mary wouldn't have had any food at all. He knew that she was totally dependent on him and on the Faculty cafeteria to prepare her food every day, for she was unable – so she claimed, at least – to prepare it in the girls' hostel. Anyway, any excuse would do when Miss Mary saw the tray of food coming. She would be eager to find out what it was, shifting the lids from the plates like a starving cat. It was enough that the Faculty cafeteria should provide free food for the Principal of the girls' hostel and not stint her, because of her formidable reputation. Here, the extra food on the tray found an inevitable fate. Jasim would eat it after the Principal had finished. The dishes would be brought straight from her room to Jasim's room, very carefully, before Sadea could get her fingers dirty eating what was left over from the two people together.

Jasim reached the cafeteria and found the messengers crammed into the entrance eager to get inside. He pushed his way between them with difficulty. He didn't think of himself as one of them at all. He found himself in the kitchen pulling the covers off the food containers inquisitively as he watched the steam rising from them. They had been got ready for Miss Mary's meal as usual. He was just about to pick up the tray and go, when one of the messengers asked him: 'Jasim, what's your news?'

'About what?'

'About the thieves.'

'Come on, you lot, get over these fantasies and delusions!'

'What? What are you saying? Are you really saying this, Jasim? Are you happy that there should be thieves, even in the girls' hostel? Where are we living? What sort of security is this? What sort of regime?'

Jasim sighed, as his anxiety left him. The policeman had lost his respect; the security he represented had disappeared. Yes, the man was right. People had been perturbed by thieves, and the police presence was a complete joke. He cheered up. His tongue would be cut out if he said what he thought about the thieves on that dark night. He wasn't going to say a word to indicate his belief that there weren't any thieves because the 'thieves' were just students. He stopped to fasten his belt. He ambled along in his new shoes as he carried the tray of food, walking slowly like a ship making its way through the Gulf.

When he entered the front garden of the hostel, he found the policeman licking a metal cup. Yogurt was sticking to his thick black moustache like a shoe brush with white polish on it. He was chewing his last date, it seemed, before stuffing the leftovers into his bag and filling himself up by drinking from the water jar. Jasim escaped from him easily. The policeman was preoccupied with his lunchtime snack, which he was eating totally calmly. He didn't ask Jasim anything, and he paid no attention to his entrance through the garden gate.

* * * * *

One of the things that made Jasim the caretaker happy was making tea for himself. He loved to bring his teapot, to line up his utensils and make his cigarette smoke dance around him. In the evening he would turn the radio on. It was a dusty radio that he had brought from the flea market. The dial wouldn't show any station except Radio Baghdad. Jasim had several times tried to find a cure for this fault but had always failed. The sound would always crackle on the other radio stations, a sort of breathing in and out like a braying donkey or a hissing of a snake. In the end he would always listen to the 'real' station, as he called it. Content with that, since it seemed loud and clear. On that station, country folk would sound off as they were supposed to, while the government would attack all and sundry, when it wanted to, with the most nonsensical statements, or else dole out praise, and brag about itself without shame or conscience. He felt better sometimes as he squatted, drawing a belching sigh, when some bad idea passed through his mind.

He would listen to the news broadcasts every day, following the course of the political ups and downs intently. He didn't take much notice when he heard about fights breaking out, or about disputes between different factions, killings, torture, executions or people put in jail, humiliated, insulted, or deprived of the most basic human rights. The word 'mercy', or the need for it, was something that was not necessary at all.

This sort of thing had finished for him long ago. He had lived his whole life from childhood to youth without any mercy worth mentioning. He was in a continuous state of emergency. He had survived diseases like bilharzia, typhoid, various sorts of fever, hunger, heat, cold, snake bites and scorpion bites, in their dark hut without water or electricity. His life had been a succession of struggles on every level. In the end it was just a struggle to stay alive. This was clearly apparent in his conversations with Master Rajab accusing other people of all sorts of things, without reservation, intent on giving the harshest verdict. In the course of his tale, he would allude in passing to his past, blaming the overseer, the agent Sayyah, for deceiving the powerless peasants by bribing an influential official who had come from the capital, Baghdad, to implement the Agricultural Reform Law in their village after the fall of the monarchy in 1958. How he had cut off the water from their fields, so that they dried out and the crops and animals died. How he had cheated them over their rations of seeds, which he had fiddled. He spoke with loathing about the former feudal landowner Ibn Fir'awn, who had visited them and attended to the land only occasionally, but was there to profit from their efforts and revenue from their husbandry at the end of the harvest. Since coming to Baghdad, Jasim's world had become broader and better than before. He had escaped from them by a miracle. He was no longer restricted to these folk or to a crowd of people like Mahidi, Na'na'a, Shamma and 'Abbas. He had come a long way to arrive at his knowledge of the names of ministers, leaders and presidents. He had become civilised, through the novel expressions that he learnt every day from his radio during the news broadcasts. He would leap up from his seat like a man on fire when the time came, at six o'clock, eight o'clock, one, and so on... he would hear important and frightening epithets relating to both individuals and groups, as it seemed. People would give each other reproachful names, like communist, Ba'athist, nationalist, Zionist, imperialist, Mason and anything else that was going. In the past, as far as he was concerned, a person was just a Shi'ite, a Sunni, Jew, Christian, Sabaean, and everything was straightforward. But this wasn't enough to divide up humankind, apparently. The adjectives today betrayed a more convulsive and painful division. He would bandy them about, splashing them around on anyone he fancied at the appropriate time, hurting people on a whim. Whether he was standing with Master Rajab or squatting on his folk carpet in his room, feeling relaxed and content by comparison with the other wretches, especially as his radio was beside him, which allowed him this free amusement in every circumstance.

    The situation had changed since the policeman came as a rival guard. Even the pleasure and scent of the tea had changed. The ring of the teaspoon would often attract the attention of policeman Hasan. The latter would hurry to him, apparently just heading towards his room but really to have tea with him. And when the conversation had run out of lions and wolves and smugglers' vehicles on the borders, and girls running away with their lovers, the policeman would talk about politics. He had a number displayed prominently on his chest, to demonstrate his significance and his status in the regime. He understood its importance and he acted in accordance with it. In short, he belittled Jasim.

'You didn't see the old Prime Minster Nuri Sa'id. *Ya, ya, ya.* I saw him with my own eyes at the door of the General Security Directorate during a private visit. He shook my hand. There were ten of us and I was standing on the left. I saw the ex- prime minister 'Abd al-Karim Qasim as well. Yes, he came to inspect us. He talked to us, and I could touch his shoulder, just like I'm touching your shoulder now. *Bah, bah, bah!*'

'I'm sorry I wasn't in the province. Unfortunately, I missed the sight of them torturing him by dragging him round the streets.'

As soon as the policeman heard the word 'torture' all his senses were alerted. He understood that Jasim was talking about Nuri Sa'id being dragged round the streets of Baghdad by the mob in 1958, when a soldier spotted him disguised in women's clothes. He wanted to stop him, but Nuri Sa'id resisted, getting out his revolver to defend himself. People passing by were disturbed, and angry groups of people, people like Jasim, rounded on him. Policeman Hasan was now burning inside himself, as he exclaimed: *wai, wai, wai*!

Jasim didn't understand anything of this. The policeman kept silent, worn out, remembering nothing except how they had taken off their official police uniforms at the time. How he and his colleagues had been afraid of being taken for people loyal to Nuri Sa'id's authority and punished for it. They had stayed out of the way in their houses, continuing to absent themselves from their stations and were anxious for several days, until they put on a new face and changed their colours. Some of them began to chant Communist Party slogans in demonstrations, adapting themselves to the new, changing situation as they believed it to be.

'Ask the policeman "what do you want?"
"A free country and a people content!" '

Hasan the policeman seized the initiative again. 'You think that everything changes. No, no, no! Everything stays just as it is. The faces and the names change, that's all!'

Jasim felt uneasy. 'And the radio?' he asked anxiously, keen not to be disappointed.

Policeman Hasan laughed so much he almost collapsed. 'You believe what the radio says?' he asked. 'You poor thing! Ha, ha, you are stupid! You only say that because you spend your whole day sitting by the door!'

Jasim's heart shrank. It was a treacherous dagger blow from behind. There was nothing left for Hasan to call him except 'You ass!' – a word he recalled being uttered repeatedly when he was at the mercy of the foreman Sayyah. The peasants didn't care even if Sayyah spat at them when he told one of them off. Sometimes, a peasant would exploit it and boast about it in front of his friends, as proof that he had not been forgotten, or gone unrecognised by this high-ranking personage whom he had met face to face.

Jasim was now stony-faced. There was no point in arguing. The policeman just had his opinion, and it would do no good to oppose it. 'Get lost!' Jasim kept muttering silently to himself. The push-and-pull effect had made advances during their periods sitting together, as he made fun of him and his radio. Little by little his enthusiasm and appetite for the radio had grown weaker. It was no longer the miracle machine, transporting him to worlds of pleasure and delight – especially when he listened to news of disturbances in Iraq with complete equanimity. He was really pleased that the traitors' reputation had been blown away; it made him feel safer and more valuable. Jasim would eagerly follow the course of their trials when they were broadcast on the radio, and a strange, obscure happiness would spread across his face. The only things that could compensate for it were reciprocal loving relationships, or the sex and love of which he had been totally deprived, ever since Naema had betrayed him. Since then he had made up for this enormous loss by a life of conspicuous chastity alongside the hostel Principal, Miss Mary, and the girl students. Following what was happening in the political arena had become his hobby, like a spectator at a horse race or football match. The winner took the seat that was being fought over. He would cheer up no end when the death sentence was announced on one of these competitors for political power. Radio Baghdad would begin, with a total lack of dignity, to heap curses and abuse on them. Yesterday's patriot would become a traitor of the first degree, and vice versa. Anyone could be humiliated by all means possible without any fear of punishment or revenge. Jasim would be the first to rush to enjoy the spectacle of people being hanged on the gallows in Freedom Square or some other public place. He would get ready to go out early, at dawn, before breakfast or prayer time. The executions seemed to him just a part of an open-air picnic for his personal enjoyment. The question of justice in sentencing, or whether people were innocent or guilty, never bothered him or even occurred to him.

The meaning of justice was totally obscure to him. It was an issue no different from the matter of mercy, something that had not existed in his own difficult life experience. Injustice had for centuries been the rule and the measure of life, without complaint or argument from him or from his folk.

* * * * *

He came back from the Faculty canteen that day in high spirits. After eating his lunch he washed his hands and began to prepare his tea things. He called to the policeman in a sing-song tone to sit down and join him:

'Would you like to have tea?' he asked.

Hasan grunted without saying yes or no, and got up from where he was sleeping. He was happy but at a loose end. He rubbed his hands together as he went towards Jasim's room, content with the magnitude of the question.

'Shall we drink it here or there?'

Jasim was beside himself with happiness. He pointed to a palm-frond chair beside him, showing concern for the policeman's state of health as he made a comfortable position ready for him in his room.

'No, no, come on here, come on, in the room!'

He drew up a chair for him with apparent affection, and contented himself with sitting on a carpet with orange-coloured folkloric patterns, a style and design unchanged since time immemorial. It was midday on a warm February day in Baghdad and the fragrance of the tea rose up, hovering in the air.

'The thieves haven't been caught yet!' Jasim had pulled out the fuse, thrown his grenade and walked away.

'No,' replied the policeman innocently, laughing broadly, unaware of the trap being set for him.

'It's really strange, thieves even in the girls' hostel!'

'There's nothing strange in this world!'

'Really? Is it credible? Is it logical?'

'Why not?'

'When did you hear of thieves breaking into a place like this?'

'Thieves are a rotten lot; they can even rob poor people's huts and homes, so why shouldn't they come here?'

'And security?'

The grenade had finally gone off. Jasim was afraid, but the policeman encouraged him: 'What do you mean?' he asked.

'I mean, what happened to security?'

'Security can't do everything. Security's not enough without other people's help.'

Jasim summoned all his powers, turning into a solid lump of malice.

'Oh come on, sir! It's strong security that makes people strong! When are you going to get beyond these excuses?'

The policeman cleared his throat and chewed half his moustache. He kicked one boot out of the way and moved the other forward. He spoke extra harshly, for he had discovered a fault in himself.

'You're a caretaker too. Are you, or aren't you?'

'Yes, of course!'

'Okay, why didn't you stop the intruders that night?'

'That's another matter!'

'How come? It's exactly the same!'

Jasim threw down all his weapons and surrendered. He took the teapot in his right hand. 'Another glass?'

'No thanks, I've had enough.'

The policeman was keeping his arrows close to his chest. He had just changed his tone. Nothing more. But despite that, Jasim recovered some of the happiness of a quarrelsome, spiteful boy. He was happy to see his enemy, the policeman, become his friend after learning of his inferiority. There was just a little way to go to see the policeman as his equal. How small the gap! His hand found pleasure in his lighted cigarette and the palm-frond chair quickly shifted a little. All at once, the policeman stood up and left the place where he was sitting, forgetting his adventures in Basra, Amara and Mosul. He was once again a failure like the others.

* * * * *

The tea session had finished as well as it could, just as Jasim had wanted. He started to gather up the tea things and wash them. He rinsed a blue *dishdasha*, then made his bed, meanwhile recalling a brown jacket he had been given by the administrative inspector in the Ministry of Education. Jasim had been his office boy for a short period before being appointed caretaker in the girls' hostel. It wasn't just a jacket, there had also been trousers made of the same material. Anyway, this didn't concern him now: trousers weren't part of his dress, they weren't one of the characteristics of a person with a tribesman's temperament, who was not going to ditch his garb or his customs in a hurry. He took the jacket out of the trunk and it seemed suitable in every sense of the word. It was new and exactly his size. He brushed its stiff folds with a little water, pressing the collar several times with his hand. Finally he put it on. He held his head up high, throwing aside his head cord and *kaffiyah* with the black and white squares that he sometimes wore. He wished he could have had smooth, flat hair, with a parting on the left, for example. And why not, Jasim? Why this neglect? What is to stop you wearing your new shoes, again, today? Wishes like these could easily be achieved while Jasim was young. Let the time of sorrow and retreat leave his brow, full of disappointment. Let Naema go. He was the one who began the separation, after he had abandoned her for three years. He had deserted her without leaving her even a single note. Let Naema go to the Devil. There were lots of other women besides her. He was free, he would marry if he wanted. His age, which had never been recorded properly, might well be around forty or even thirty. This wasn't the important thing, so why think about it? He put his *kaffiyah* back on his head hoping for the best.

He hadn't been sitting by the door for long before Sadea called him and asked him to look at a fault in the bath tap. It was Thursday. The boarding girls, most of them anyway, usually took a bath on Thursday, making the most of the weekly Friday holiday as they got ready to go out, to enjoy an escape from their serious, regular lessons. At these times, Jasim would bring oil from the big barrel outside, and light a fire in an opening on the wall of the building, with a big tank above it, with pipes that led to the baths. The warm water would flow, and Jasim would then usually call out loud to the girl in the bathroom waiting to begin washing. 'Has the water come through?'

'Yes, it's come', the girl would answer from inside, without his knowing who it was, or else she would call out imploringly: 'No, no, it's still cold.'

Jasim would continue the operation, pumping the oil to make the fire burn more vigorously, and the tank would start to boil. Jasim was used to being the sole person in charge of this daily heating operation: he would stand with his sleeves rolled up waiting for the hot water to reach the girl, until he was finally happy about her and could relax. Today, as requested, he went to check the top of the tap, which had come loose, while the hot water carried on bubbling and steaming away. A girl was standing waiting, holding her clothes over her chest. Jasim brought a bucket and put it under the tap, straightening the tap with all the power and force at his disposal. He straightened it by repeatedly pressing on it, then adjusted the temperature of the hot water, mixing it with cold. Two taps flowed into the wash tub, ready for whoever wanted to bathe that day to step under them. The girl hurriedly appeared, and quickly put her clothes on a shelf inside the bathroom. She took the soap, ready to take off her underclothes before washing. Jasim wanted to hear her voice, after he had stood up in confusion, but could only hear the sound of the water. He checked that it was a moderate temperature for the first time as he touched it. Jasim did what he had to with a smile and went out of the bathroom, closing the door behind him.

He passed by the girls in the spacious entrance room. They were sitting talking among themselves in loud voices. Conversation, smiles and laughter. They should notice his coffee-coloured jacket and his shining new shoes. Any fault he still had, he would correct it. He went to the entrance to sit with the policeman. Jasim found Hasan, his eyes lifeless, sitting, standing, or walking along the garden path. For the first time since he had known him he found him agreeable. Jasim called him cheerily, happy to meet him. They sat together like two allies in protecting the girls. Jasim began to hone his skills and tell him what he knew. He was afraid he might forget to tell Hasan that Sadea was afraid of him, for, by chance, she was passing the door. And Miss Mary was more compliant even than his own fingertips. She wanted his advice in times of need, and when she travelled to her family in Mosul on her days off, she left all the hostel keys with him. She had brought him a red woollen Bedouin carpet as a present; she had come to his room to enquire about him when he had a cold last winter. She would have sat down on his bed, had she not been a woman and it would have been a shameful thing to do. She was jealous of the girls. Miss Mary put lotion on her face in the evening and wiped it off in the day. She was angry when Sadea talked to Jasim. She believed that Sadea was in love with him, when God knew that his relations with Sadea were like brother and sister. It was true that she bickered with him and tried to get close to him, but he personally had no interest in her. It was the same with all the girls. He didn't give them any opportunity – or else, brother Hasan, you would see that they weren't all so chaste or goody-goody.

What had he forgotten, what had he left out? There were lots of things to talk about, too many to finish in one session. The policeman found the conversation gentle, affecting and tantalising. The smugglers' vehicles, the robbers, the adventure trying to stamp out the criminal killers, all seemed unimportant, trivial and bland, compared with these delightful little problems – soft, tasty sweetmeats that made the mouth water. His weakness was apparent for all to see. Hasan the policeman's presence was unnecessary here, despite his interruptions and his habit of butting in on things that didn't concern him about the hostel and Miss Mary's merits. From that day on, however, his place had become threatened, his existence like a void. He felt cold, and found an excuse to go to the cubbyhole where his bed was. And Jasim also asked him, politely and quite happily, to fetch Miss Mary's supper from the Faculty café.

* * * * *

The caretaker spent a carefree evening, as if Naema had never left him, or even existed, occupying himself with his own personal affairs. He thought about the coffee-coloured trousers, the neglected companion of the jacket in the trunk. He took them out, like someone hauling in fish on a hook. The trouser legs lay stretched out on the bed, pressed flat to get rid of the creases. It was good that the trousers matched the jacket, and were the same colour and material. He quickly took off his *dishdasha*, almost removing his head in the process, then thrust first one foot, then the other, into the trouser legs. He examined himself from every angle as he turned around. No, no, not a blemish in sight. Exactly the right style and cut. Except that a slight unease had suddenly come over him. No, he didn't want to declare war on the customs of his people, the Dabha tribe. He remembered his cousin Juma, his uncle Hilayyil and his uncle Mazal. He knew what annoyed them and made them angry. It was certainly jealousy, he knew that very well. He wouldn't go to them in his new costume, for there would be lots of outbursts or comments to harm him. People were ignorant, they didn't know that was appropriate for him in Baghdad; they didn't know the importance of the right lifestyle. In short, they envied him his position. When he had visited him last summer and gone into his room, Muhaysin had said to him: 'Your water's pure and your shadow solid, what do you ask for in your prayers, Jasim?' Yes, these people, this was their mentality, they were always after him and wouldn't leave him alone. How could they understand his important role in Baghdad, when they were hundreds of miles away? How could they understand him – these people who are still living in one room with their chickens and buffaloes? When it rained, the roof would fall down on them and their wives had to go outside with them to patch up the holes at the last minute. Yes, they were jealous of him. He was not going to pander to their ideas. He'd had enough. He was a proper employee now, with a regular monthly salary. He was responsible for appearing smart in front of other people, in order to gain respect.

* * * * *

He felt refreshed in spirit as he finally sat down. Hasan saw him and shouted to him from his cubbyhole, astonished beyond reason at the change in what he was wearing. 'Hey, are you in a suit?'

Jasim smiled in contempt: 'God curse you, do you think you're the only one who can look respectable?'

The girls going through the exit door noticed Jasim in trousers, and he thought they seemed happy. His embarrassment subsided. He felt grand as Sadea called him. He disappeared inside the building with his new trousers. Things were generally going fine. He stood straighter as he walked. The trousers didn't flap between his legs like a *dishdasha*. He was in a daze as he walked along, and if it hadn't been for falling over a blind chair he would have thought that his job had all the blessings, and that the policeman's arrival to keep him company in his caretaking job had been a gift from Heaven.

'You've done well, Jasim!' thought Miss Mary, giving him a glance of approval at his new outfit. He, as it were, walked on four legs, two of them foreign. It took a little time to get used to trotting on just two. His shoes took on a new lease of life and he stood taller. He went out to meet the laundryman Salman in his shop nearby, showing off half his body. Salman was busy ironing. He raised his eyebrows and gave a long whistle, he was so surprised. As the material in front of him began to steam, he shouted out, trying to attract the attention of Master Rajab in the shop opposite, exchanging with him a coarse joke of admiration. Jasim carried on laughing stupidly, and continued to laugh until the laughter turned into a snort. When he had finished, he told Master Rajab that he had tasks to accomplish, then explaining that he just wanted to go to the canteen, that was all. He walked about happily, up and down, on top of the world, and everyone who saw him thought there was no one else like him.

He was so preoccupied with his own affairs that day that he didn't bother about the policeman except when he made him aware of his presence. Several times Jasim slumped down on his chair, swinging his legs like branches. He discovered that there were several girls who wanted to laugh with him. He returned the compliment, bought things for some of them, and listened at the closed doors of their rooms. Are they talking about me? Perhaps Siham in this room, or Leila or Wahida in that, would mention him? He realised that he had never paid any attention to them before. Now he felt himself aching with longing for Wahida. He stood about here and there, going to their doors and greeting them; they were weak but close by, pure and secure. He wished their demands would mean he could stand there longer. He went down from the upper floor burning with lust, the near-dead ashes of his heart throbbing hard, till he was blazing like a torch. He made for his room in the garden, passing the green plants that had become dejected the evening he was sad and in pain. He wished he could cry into the lap of his bed and that the policeman would run to him to console him rather than torment him. He would then complain to him of the agonies of loneliness, cowardice, sexual deprivation, and the cruelty of having to guard and protect the girls he was really dying to have.

Chapter Two

The dormitory has six large rooms inhabited by thirty-five girls. Miss Mary's room is on the right hand side of the building. It has four armchairs, besides an Indian oak wood bedstead, covered with embroidered sheets and new blankets. After Miss Mary uses them first, these blankets are put on the girl's beds later.

A photograph hanging in the middle of the wall, facing the room's entrance, testifies to Miss Mary's great passion; it is of her late husband. Alongside it hang photographs of her nephew, Hakmat and her Auntie Najiba. All three photographs spread an atmosphere of cosiness and domestication for everyone inside the dormitory. It is home to them all, except for the cleaner, Sadea. Her work in the dormitory entitles her to stay there only during the day. She comes every morning to clean the rooms, mop the stairs and bathrooms, and look after Miss Mary and the girls. When she finishes at six o'clock in the evening she goes home, having only had a small light lunch; normally consisting of whatever was left over, or a simple dip. She leaves the dormitory and walks to take the first bus, then changes to a second bus which takes her straight to her brother's house in the al-Kadhim district. It is the custom and tradition that women cannot live alone. They live with their relatives all their life, till they get married. It occurred to Sadea, many times, that she would like to be able to move her brother's home nearer to her work. She was unable to voice this wish openly to him, as he emphatically refused to move from the al-Kadhim district, which was more convenient for his job. In the end she surrendered and gave up the idea of moving home, accepting her fate passively. She knew very well that he thought that she should quit her job altogether, instead of changing his home unnecessarily.

However, despite the long distance between the dormitory and her home, Sadea managed to stay in her job, with its regular working hours, without objection. Throughout, she respected Miss Mary's orders and the girls and seldom disobeyed the caretaker, Jasim. In time, her existence in the dormitory, which had no significance for her personally, became part of her life, more important to her than her brother's distant home. For her part, her sister-in-law found Sadea's absence at work convenient. She was rid of her at last, relieved that she had no rival in the house, where perhaps one might like to do something while the other wanted to do the opposite.

From the first day Jasim started work in the dormitory, Sadea sympathized with him. She listened to his complaints many times, when he came to her distressed and moaning. He used to think that he was the only person taken advantage of in the whole place. He kept criticizing Miss Mary, whom he considered to have the most comfortable position in the whole building, while nobody suffered like him and Sadea. He would grumble to her while sometimes bringing socks with holes to darn or a jacket with split seams to mend, unable to get the thread into the needle.

He could not imagine how it was possible to do all this sewing; he concluded it was a really hard job. Sadea, without fuss, sewed whatever he brought to her, with kindness and care. She told him later not to hesitate to ask if he felt in need of assistance, especially when she was always there. For some reason she kept thinking that he needed her, as if he was new to his job, despite all the years he had spent living with them in the dormitory. She had always felt that way since the old caretaker Hajj Ali died in his sleep, and she had found his body in his room one morning. Since then, she felt she had more responsibility and experience than Jasim, who arrived within a week of Hajj Ali's death, when the Ministry of Education replaced him. She had never changed her mind since then about him. Jasim arrived shy and coy; to take up his job and could not even dare to look her in the eye. Miss Mary, after introducing him, said to her: 'show him his room'. Sadea walked in front of him, in order to lead the way towards the isolated room in the garden.

As the door of the room opened, they found Hajj Ali's empty old bed. His pair of sandals lay there, and a rag had fallen on the floor beside them. Hajj Ali used to tie this piece of cloth around his stomach when the pain became unbearable. Immediately Sadea felt sorry for Jasim. He was young compared to Hajj Ali. Jasim would be fearful and alarmed if she left him alone, she thought. Standing by the door, she chatted with him, as a form of consolation. Then she asked him his name and which town he came from, laughing with surprise when he told her that he came to Baghdad to run away from his relatives. She found in him a sign of honesty and frankness, and hurried to make tea for him, hoping to increase his cheerfulness and comfort. He thanked her as he arranged his belongings in this neglected room, preparing conscientiously to carry out the duties of the job.

Things went along ship-shape between them. Not one day of vexation. Even when Jasim treated her badly she was unable to behave likewise to him. Lately, he had started to come to her in the kitchen, upset and bothered, annoyed and troubled, all because of the policeman. He told her, nervously, that the policeman's eyes were always fixed on the girls' comings and goings. Always wickedly whispering dirty jokes about them. He was determined to inform Miss Mary about all this; it was time to get rid of the policeman for good. Send him back to where he came from. It needed some one to punish him by sacking him from his job or at least kick him out of the dormitory itself. Sadea looked at him, surprised and bewildered, inquiring about the whole thing:

"But he is not in the building, he is outside."

"Never mind. Haven't you noticed how he stares at the whole dormitory? Didn't you see his face? Guess his intentions?"

"And do you know his intentions?" Sadea questioned him again.

He answered her abruptly, cynical, questioning her in return, bluntly:

"Don't you know that yourself?"

She was left scared, standing near him cautiously holding the bucket of water for cleaning the floor of the hall, for fear of spilling it.

* * * * *

The affairs of the dormitory started to settle down. Jasim said the policeman would go. The latter took his belongings and his folding bed while some of the boarding girls stood behind the windows witnessing his departure. He had been notified that the danger was over, gone at last, and there was no necessity for a policeman to stay any longer. A khaki jeep drew up in front of the dormitory; and he threw in his trunk and his folding bed. That done, after he said his farewells to the caretaker, Jasim, shaking his hand and hugging him around the shoulders with many kisses, he finally climbed into the back of the Jeep, waving to Jasim. The road echoed with silence, the Jeep disappeared and Jasim returned to the wide, welcoming entrance. He called upon Sadea to bring the broom, in order to clean the policeman's empty corner and what he had left behind, his cigarette butts and his garbage. His traces were completely gone. The place returned to its old shape, before the imagined burglary and everything that had followed it.

Now, the dormitory became Jasim's own domain again, as if the task of guarding it had become his inheritance. From now on he began to lift his eyes, searchingly looking at the windows above, finding excuses to go inside. When required to light the gas boiler, which was on the outside wall, he would speculate longingly, trying to find out who was inside, washing in the bath. When Sadea told him to fire up boiler he would ask inquisitively:

"And who is going to have a bath? Yesterday the fire was blazing when Salma and then afterwards Wahida were washing. Or is it someone else?" He tried to pretend to correct his mistake. Sadea would reply, to satisfy his curiosity. She would tell him in great detail who was washing, who was sleeping, who was eating. His smile would widen and his lashes would flutter.

In the kitchen, the 'orphan' found shelter near Sadea. He acted infatuated, sitting there talking, puffing out his chest, sharing her plate of food. Telling her about his past, the present and the future. Imperceptibly their relationship became less formal. Sadea started to call him by diminutives or nicknames. She started to enter his room without permission, and when laughing she would put her hand on his shoulder. In return he would jostle her from behind, throwing pieces of nut shell, which made him excited. The naïve Sadea, who was the last one to understand, became aware of what was going on. In the meantime, her eyes took on a sparkle. She started to wash her face twice a day, and wrapped her head in her black headscarf, intentionally exposing her left ear showing an imitation earring. Now and then when she entered the bathroom and there was no-one else there she began to scrub her rough feet to beautify herself. During that time the doors were open in daytime and closed at night. The girls drew their curtains at dusk, gathering them together in the dark without a gap, in case there was an opening between them allowing a thief to have a glimpse inside.

* * * * *

April came all at once. Spring exposed the girl's shoulders and bosoms. Jasim was kept busy coming and going to the laundry shop, carrying the girl's light summer dresses looking like Japanese fans. These bundles of clothes kept arriving for him, except Wahida's clothes, which never yet came to him. Once when she was passing by he threw her a remark on the hot weather, completely losing his patience after waiting for her so long. The remark carried implied meaning, although it sounded innocent:

"Summer has arrived." He uttered this short sentence without hesitation, thinking she was sweating, which he felt was enough in reply to his comment. It did not take long. Only a week later she handed him her clothes in a bag, asking him to take them to the laundry at last. He jumped up, full of excitement; his ears starting to buzz strangely. He took the bundle to his room. There it was hugged, as if he was hugging a lover. By opening, panic-stricken, the buttons of the dress he played with the sleeves, the waistband and the hem, inhaling the aroma of the material and its marvellous scent. Jasim feared Sadea might burst in on him. Coming at this hour, as has been her habit these recent days. To burst in unexpectedly, at this minute, she would see him, oblivious, in his flirtatious manner, his failure, exposing his two thighs and the dress in between them. She would discover the weakness he was hiding, unable to help it. An earthquake would be less damaging. Finally he hugged the dress with all his might. Imagining Wahida in the room with him, he wanted to cry in front of her and apologize. Take off her shoes and kiss her feet. He would not care if she spat on him. Even her spitting would hardly cause any offence to him.

* * * * *

The laundry man Salman said, while he was busy ironing:

"Tomorrow, I will wash and iron it."

Anxious at the delay, Jasim was baffled and frustrated, afflicted with extreme fear. How could he leave the dress with Salman? Could he allow it to be alone here? Looking at Salman, on the verge of tears, Jasim gabbled hurriedly, affirming the need to get it back, now, pleading for kindness and mercy:

"I beg you, I beg you, be quick, be quick, the girl wants it immediately."

Salman refused his earnest entreaty. He denied Jasim's request, saying carelessly with his mouth full of chewing gum: "Tell her it will be ready tomorrow. Enough, enough" so no one would argue with him. Pleased with his decision, the way an emperor would say it with the utmost carelessness. Jasim was bewildered. How could one convince or persuade such a horrible person? Jasim discovered while he was talking to him that he was not a virtuous man. His walls were covered with pictures of naked women's bodies cut from magazines. Pictures or photographs of disreputable dancers hung around him as well. His radio played nonstop, shameless songs. In addition, he had a vulgar gold tooth in his mouth. Jasim never noticed it before, and it showed when he laughed cheekily now. No, no; no decency here. With a heavy heart Jasim left him, hating everything he passed, including a sign on Master Rajab's shop designed to avert people's envy, as was the custom there, to prevent bad luck for the prosperous shops. The words on the wooden sign said: 'This is from God's Grace'. Jasim ridiculed him, mumbling: 'Who said you stole it?' At that moment a messenger passing by, seeing Jasim's mouth opening, thought he was greeting him.

* * * * *

At lunch, Miss Mary was lifting the cover of one of the plates on her lunch tray, saying: "Fish?" It seemed she was fed up with the dish of the day. Jasim answered, somehow trying to appease her, "Fish is nice, if not for its smell." He wanted to find out if she knew anything! Had she smelt what was cooking in his room? Miss Mary got up to wash her hands, bracelets jingling. Slowly her fat eyes looked everywhere around. Though in her mind, at that moment, there was no suspicion.

* * * * *

Jasim strode through the Medan and Haidarkana district, entering Rasheed Street. Would he continue his walk or go back? Every moment that went by, he might lose sight of the two girls. He was not satisfied with simply sitting at the doorstep. His ambition had increased now. He was going to catch up, almost, with Wahida and Salma's steps. Gathering all his endurance and patience, he wanted to know and discover the girl's world when they left his domain, Wahida's world especially.

Like birds escaping the cage, the girls eluded his grasp. The time was evening. There was no clear purpose, in his mind, for them to go out to a place called college or library. Sitting on his chair, he was dozing. As they came out of the front door near him, he felt they were running away from him. In his imagination, he pictured their intention as going out to faraway places, to strange places, where day is night and night is day, as he saw it. He decided to follow them. His aim was to pursue their traces, the way the Bedouin follows his camel's tracks in the desert. Miss Mary stood in his way, starting to nag him. She said:

"And when are you coming back?"

"I do not know, it all depends on my barber. However, I will hurry him up, to get back as soon as I can." To silence her was what he wanted, at any cost.

He wanted her to leave him alone; at last he managed to shut her up. It was his priority now to get away from her. His face was flushed as he waited at the bus stop where the two girls were standing. Sneakily, he managed to stand there behind a lamppost, hiding his face as much as he could, getting a good view of them at the same time. When the bus came they got on. Jasim followed, very aware of his trousers clinging to his legs. His long neck was as stiff as a rod, and a ten *fils* piece for the bus conductor was clutched in his hand. At the Bab al-Moadham area the bus door opened and the two girls got out. Their skirts floated in the air, driving Jasim mad. He did not waste much time, but started to follow them like a dog, hiding behind walls. Forgetting the barber, which he had fabricated as an excuse for Miss Mary in order to get out of the dormitory. He forgot the early evening, the supper, the doorstep. Finally he found himself standing near a cinema building, bewildered, penniless, alone. The two girls quickly entered the building. He looked around confused. No money in his pocket apart from two *dirhams*, no more. Was this enough to get in? Would they allow him to pass its door? Could he enter such a grand place, where people go inside silently, as though they were princes? Anyone who disobeys the order of the usher in the doorway will be hunted down. He looked around, searching for what was left of the two girls inside, finding no trace of them. He become suddenly aware it was suppertime. Jasim began to think of Miss Mary, the tray, and so on. Realizing the time of day, he decided to return to the dormitory empty-handed.

The students had already eaten in the restaurant and left. A clumsy messenger was sucking a bone in the corner. Noisily the cook was busy washing his plates. Once again, Jasim double-checked for Miss Mary's supper tray and found it on top of one of the shelves. He grabbed it quickly, lifting it up above his shoulders.

Miss Mary said almost angrily:

"Where have you been?"

He felt that lying would not buy him any time; it would be useless, to no avail. The razor had obviously never touched his hair. Miss Mary would notice herself that he had not been to the barbers. He stood, smiling, hiding his embarrassment. Miss Mary was busy now, looking at her supper tray, forgetting everything except that the food was baked beans, her favourite dish, which she loved.

After a dismal, gloomy night, Jasim fell asleep, exhausted. Just before dawn, he dreamt he was running along ancient roads and someone behind him was throwing stones at him. He felt he was falling down a well. His clothes were wet and Naema was consoling him. He saw her the way she was eight years ago; her clothes were blue and her black hair in the dark was blue also. Jasim pushed her away from him, with aversion, and she fall back again in the water. White foam spread everywhere, before a big, heavy stone fell on them both, making them start struggling together. He felt he was going to die, but unable to yell for help. Terrified, he woke from his sleep. His whole body was sweating; the smell of the room was repugnant. Quickly, he got up from his bed to put on his trousers, hiding his *dishdasha* under his pillow, his sandals concealed under the bed. Emerging from his room, he went to find Miss Mary sitting in the hall. She was busy knitting a woollen sock for her sister's grandson, trying to make sure that the measurement of the sock was right for a four-month old baby. Jasim greeted her with "good morning." Though in his heart of hearts, he did not mean it. Heading towards the kitchen he said:

"Where is the tea?" questioning and rebuking Sadea.

"I washed the teapot, would you like me to make you a fresh one?"

Answering him quickly, Sadea appeared to placate him, asking his forgiveness, as though she had been waiting for him a long time. Hiding a bucket of dirty water in the corner, she wiped her palms on the sides of her dress, and busied herself with opening a jar. Sitting upright at the table, he said:

"And the bread?"

"There is no bread here, do you want me to get you some, from Master Rajab's shop?"

"No, no need for that now."

Obstinate and annoyed, he answered her sharply. She was supposed, since they started to eat together lately, to prepare it. How could she forget his breakfast, she must know that. It was her responsibility alone now. With his fingers playing with his amber worry-beads first, then starting to open his tobacco box, he lit a cigarette and said:

"If you want good bread, you have to go to the women of my Dabha tribe."

"And do they bake their bread there?"

"Of course, we do not like the bread from the market."

"My bread is round and delicious. I am sure, if I baked it, you would find that."

It became obvious that Sadea, one day, would make it for him. Courteously and pleasantly, he began recounting the deeds of his tribe. He told her about his old past life. His grandfather was the tribal Sheikh. They had a lot of cows and buffalos. They ate butter in the morning.

Sadea opened her mouth with admiration, then inquired:

"And your cow, where did you leave it?!"

"With them, with my brother Muhsen, and my cousin Khamees. We are a big tribe; there are more than five hundred of us."

Sadea remembered she had nobody, or rather, only one. That was her brother Abood. She could not get married because of his objection to the men that came to ask for her hand – the reason being that they were inferior to him in class and position. If he had agreed she could have got married and started a family. She would bake bread for them with her own hands. Her sister-in-law started to be pessimistic after the birth of her daughter Zahra, worried she would become like her ill-fated aunt, as the saying goes. Although it was a well-known fact that Sadea's sister-in-law herself, seven years ago, waged war on the cotton carder, Mullah Hamadi, preventing Sadea from getting married to him when he asked for her hand. His job, she claimed, made the cotton stick to his beard, and she constantly made fun of him in the house, until Sadea lost all hope of such a marriage. Her brother finally clarified the matter by saying:

"Sadea, there are three kinds of people we do not get involved with in marriage; the cotton carder, the road sweeper and the lavatory cleaner." The laughter increased among them, discussing the three jobs with contempt and ridicule. Sadea bowed her head, listening to them. She was still thinking until now, why this ill-will towards them? Why do they take spiteful pleasure in the mishaps of another, who relieves them of their dirt? She kept quiet, lowering her head, thinking of how ungrateful people can be, sitting laughing around her, with no hope left that they would respect and value the sacrifice of others.

Jasim's habit in those days, when he got up, was to shake the legs of his trousers, moving his body like a dagger in its sheath. He told Sadea he was going to work. Sadea knew he was going to sit at the doorstep.

* * * * *

Water, in Baghdad's dry summer months from May onwards, makes the place closer to what is described in Islam as a promised paradise. Sadea mopped the halls with a rag, spraying water on the patio, then turned her attention to the paths of the garden. A delicate grass scent spread through the air, while the shining green colour of the trees intensified.

Sitting in the hall, Miss Mary lifted her feet so that Sadea could wipe the dust from underneath her seat with the mop. Jasim, in turn, did the same, putting his feet up on his chair in the doorway, so her hands could pass underneath it, reaching the furthest spot. She continued her work, mopping the corners and the middle of the place persistently, busying herself strenuously as though she was fighting a battle of her own. Sometimes her dress rode up more than intended.

"Have you finished?" Jasim asked her fondly.

Straightening up, she answered him, holding her breath, tired:

"All that's left is that spot."

"I'll buy us some cold juice," Jasim promised her in a friendly way.

Her eyes shone with happiness at the suggestion. Her fingers gathered to undo the knot in her headscarf in order to get at her money hidden there. He entreated her earnestly, protesting his refusal strongly, insisting:

"Not at all, I'll buy it with my own money." He was determined to make her drink with him as his treat. Standing up straight in his new clothes, heading towards the shop of Master Rajab, as though it was Adam going out to hunt for food, leaving Eve waiting.

* * * * *

Sadea threw down the mop with delight. She laid the broomstick to one side in the kitchen, then put down a rug. She felt this place had become her own real home as, at that moment, she hunted for other slippers to change into instead of the old battered ones she was wearing. Jasim soon returned, finding her appearing clean and dry with blooming cheeks in front of him. Putting two ice cream tubs on the table, he said:

"Come and sit on a chair; let's eat here." When she didn't object he sat in front of her, and both of them started to lick from the two ice creams tubs. The heat made the soft ice melt quickly. They continued licking, until Miss Mary roared like a lion from inside the building. It sounded as if somebody had disobeyed her request by not carrying it out at once:

"Sadea?"

The latter started. Jasim ridiculed Miss Mary in disgust, seeing his companion leaving the ice cream tub, getting up and hurrying out. He said:

"The Governess is working."

Miss Mary came up to them. Before anyone could disobey her order, she asked Sadea harshly:

"Did you finish cleaning the garden patio?"

"I'll do it now."

Overhearing Sadea's yielding, Jasim prepared to help her in her task. He held the water hose in both hands, the other end attached to the tap. As he co-operated with her, water started to flow abundantly, sparkling around in the process. Splashes reached her face before she realized that he was himself directing the water hose towards her. It was only horseplay; she laughed with him through the water, unable to hide her enjoyment and merriment. Jasim said, as they anticipated what was coming:

"When do the holidays start?"

"Not long now."

"A month?"

"Less."

"And when does Miss Mary leave, may God take her life?"

"Two weeks after the holidays start."

"And will you be coming to the dormitory yourself during the holiday?"

"Just a week or ten days before the start of the new term," she sighed.

Miss Mary could be glimpsed standing at the doorway looking out over the garden. The conversation between Jasim and Sadea was cut short. Sadea was afraid of hearing the roar again. Miss Mary was ordering Jasim, this time, to bring six blocks of soap quickly to the dormitory.

* * * * *

The end of the year was fast drawing near. The girls wandered around restlessly reading aloud in groups or by themselves for their final examinations. Some of them, to be alone, would go up to the flat roof of the building, getting away from the noise. They would either lean against the walls or lie on their fronts or backs. The curtains started to be left undrawn, without any fear, because of the intense heat at night, the girls feeling unconsciously that they were safe from the thieves now. The heat took their apprehension away. Jasim was often asked by them to bring cold juices from Master Rajab. Empty bottles turned up all over the building, causing Jasim to go up and down, searching everywhere for the discarded containers. Meanwhile, he suffered agonies from seeing the girls everywhere he looked. Whether the girl was Wahida or not Wahida, the effect was the same. All these girls had become to him one singular woman. In a week or two, when departure became imminent, there was a great danger that he was going to lose them all at once. He had the feeling of ever-approaching separation.

Suddenly, one of the girls, when she could not find her underwear hanging on the washing line on the roof terrace, said in surprise to another:

"Have you seen it?"

"No."

"I hung it out myself, where can it be?"

"What colour is it?"

"Green."

"Ask the other girls, perhaps it got mixed up with their clothes."

She searched here and there and could not find it. Soon inquiries started among Mayada, Suad, Layla and many others, all looking for their underwear, which had been hung up in the same way and which had vanished, leaving them confused and bewildered. Suad advised them, sensibly:

"Do you know that crows steal things?"

Their mouths dropped in surprise, as they said with one voice:

"*Do* crows steal?"

"Yes!"

One of them approached the group, wanting to explain, while eating an apple:

"It's true. My mother told me that one day, when she was nursing my small sister inside the mosquito net on the rooftop at dawn, she saw a crow swoop down on the wash basin near her and grab the soap."

Hearing this tale they suddenly started to laugh out loud, surprised at the craftiness of the small, black bird. They would forgive him even though he was a thief. The subject was completely forgotten by them after a while, as they busied themselves with other affairs. Suad put on a very dark red colour lipstick which she had bought recently, she told them, from River Street. Her colleague took it from her to examine it carefully, asking permission to try it on herself first, hoping she could also buy one before she left.

Finally, the day of departure arrived. A car came at noon to take five girls all at once. Jasim brought their luggage to the car, feeling distressed. The number of girls in the rooms started to diminish. Silence echoed, emptiness prevailed. Car after car came to take them all away with their belongings. Only one or two remained for another two days. The whole dormitory lost its girls on a daily basis, including Jasim's beloved Wahida. He was forced to hide his feelings and ruthlessly stifle his dreams about them. At the end of the week he faced Miss Mary preparing herself likewise to depart. He ask her woefully:

"Where are you going this year?"

"I am going to Lebanon. It's nice in the summer."

Jasim was disappointed. Such a large sum to enter a nightclub upset him, the huge amount preventing him from seeing Lully. He said, injured:

"Not much!" He started to count dismally on his fingers. Salman defended his opinion with a trite comment:

"Everything has its price."

"Right, I know."

With humility, Jasim agreed. They were sure the price would not be reduced. She certainly merited every penny. In no time Jasim brightened up, making a pact with Salman as he accepted the offer as soon as the latter asked if he would like to go with him.

Jasim started to imagine how he would enjoy seeing Lully. How she would fall in love with him, become amorous and so on. He did not forget that Salman would be jealous. He would be forgiven. After all, Lully was in love with Salman first, before she even knew Jasim. Who knows, she might reduce her fee, accepting less than her value, as she would be passionately in love with him. Perhaps she might even be free, for him, sometimes. Pleased with himself, he felt he was somehow lucky, finding an easy prey like Lully.

Salman in his turn began to describe parts of her body. Mentioning her stunning eyes, her stature, and her treasure trove of assets and graces. Impatiently, Jasim could not wait for the coming Thursday, when Salman had offered to take him to her. They were setting off early to see her. Jasim was waiting eagerly for the time to come and spent ages varnishing his red shoes with the shoe polish that he found left behind on the floor of the girls' rooms. He had also bought a new necktie for fifty *fils*. In the meantime, he breathlessly collected more information about her, promising himself to make every bit of her body dance and shake in front of him. With brilliant revenge, he would not leave a single one of her limbs able to move without shaking.

At noon on the promised day, the Baghdad August sun hit the tarmac vertically, hissing on the pavement as usual with its vicious hot steam. Despite that, Jasim needed the sun desperately, to help him to know the correct time. He locked his room, as well as the rest of the doors. Making sure they were all shut, he went out of the dormitory. He did not regret going out early to be on the safe side. By the walls he was shaded, away from the tyranny of the heat and sun. Waiting for Salman became easy, as he found enough shelter in the big bus garage there. The buses kept coming and going from the same spot in Bab al-Moadham Square. With a sidelong glance he saw a clock indicating four o'clock in the afternoon, and kept circling around it. He went to and fro, drank a currant juice standing up, unable to make a final decision to enter one of the nearby cafes for fear of the expense. Finally he squatted on the ground and waited. The café, in his opinion, was only a waste of money on such a day: every *dirham* was precious to him, to be spent only on the utmost necessity. He moved to sit on the doorstep of a furniture shop, looking inside through the window, feeling that its seats must surely be very comfortable, thinking that he had to wait until sunset. Salman arrived in a hurry at six o'clock, fanning the heat from his face, upset with the dead watch on his wrist, as he said. Looking at it, its golden strap glittered, Jasim smelt cologne on him, mixed with copious sweat. Salman had certainly prepared himself to meet Lully. His open-necked shirt revealed his hairy chest, and his shaven face concealed a secret. The guide felt obliged to complete his impending duty. With confidence and friendliness he shook hands warmly with Jasim. Heading off to the promised nightclub, they got on the bus, both relying on his superior knowledge and intelligence. Some distance along the road they got off at a bus stop. One of the shoes they were wearing started to squeak loudly, but nobody took any notice of it. Salman pointed to a dot faraway, telling Jasim to look at it carefully. It was the nightclub, hiding as if shy behind an old eucalyptus tree, covering its private parts. With the air of an old hand, Salman went forward to buy tickets for them at the door. They both entered the auditorium with rapture. Jasim held half a *dinar* in his hand, the change he was given with the ticket, forgetting to count it when it was returned to him. Both of them took a seat in a place very near to the stage, as they were the first to arrive. They looked at the faraway tables, spread with white linen tablecloths; pointing to the empty chairs, Jasim commented:

"The nightclub is empty."

"The fans have not arrived yet, it's still early."

As Salman expected, it did not take long for the seats to fill up. Some of the patrons were carrying bottles of alcohol, others contented themselves with glasses they ordered, put on the table in front of them. Salman called boldly to somebody:

"Matty!"

The waiter Matty came over, dancing as he walked, holding up a tray in his hand. His white jacket was tight, a black bow tie nearly suffocating him at the neck. Salman said to him, without any respect:

"Quarter of a glass of *arrack* for each of us."

Matty moved away with his dancing walk again, finding it easy to move among the tables and chairs, sleek as a reptile. With the face of one satisfied at fulfilling his promise, Salman inquired from Jasim contentedly:

"So?"

"And where is Lully?"

"The man cannot wait for Lully! He is in a hurry!" Salman answered him playfully. He calmed him down delightedly, laughing together, enchanted. Jasim understood implicitly that Lully would arrive any minute; his silence mellowed greatly as he drank the quarter of *arrack* in front of him. Salman also drank his share, asking Matty again and again for more of the liquid. People started to enter the place, gradually, dragging the chairs from underneath the tables, with politeness and relish, taking sips from their glasses. The smell of *arrack* spread. One drinker disputed over a chair with another. The battle subsided, with heavy swearing, the way it had started. Jasim was frightened for a while, when the auditorium started to become agitated again. Clapping and whistling began. The curtains on the stage started to draw back, slowly, revealing the secret of its artifice and craft. Jasim inquired worriedly, leaning over to his companion's side, wistfully:

"Is the show starting?"

Salman reassured him with a big smile:

"Yes, by your father's grave, I swear."

Jasim felt obliged to match Salman's mood, the alcohol working profoundly on both. He swore, likewise, retaliating with laughter:

"And the whole of my tribe will be sacrificed for you."

Two girls appeared on the stage, singing in unison, doing their best to amuse the audience with their artless flowing movements. They finished squeakily, and the bored audience was relieved to get rid of them. Just out of courtesy, the patrons clapped, casually. Jasim kept on nagging:

"And where is Lully?"

"In a minute; this is all an appetizer for Lully!"

Jasim was amused and delighted:

"Is she only the dessert?"

Salman answered him with utmost pleasure:

"She is pure sweet sugary fruit!"

It was obvious the alcohol was playing with Salman's head, and his evident intoxication was manifesting itself. On the stage the presenter again appeared, to announce the second turn. He added to the waiting audience that the one who would be coming on was Lully, and you know very well who Lully is. Shouting started cheerfully, everyone in the crowd joining together, yelling in one voice:

"Lully!"

The audience started saying 'Allah Akbar' mixed with halleluiahs. At last, the curtain drew back slowly as if it was reluctant to open. Salman got up from his seat, overwhelmed with emotion, standing up to applaud. Other men straightened up like statues, doing the same thing beside, behind and in front of him. The crowd was engulfed in repeated clapping, sometimes serious, and other times laughing. Jasim was lost in between, not knowing what to do; should he stand up or sit down, be silent or shout? In the end, his shock subsiding, he decided to applaud strongly with the rest of them, until they all got tired and returned to their places.

Lully appeared on the stage, boldly flaunting her presence there. She walked flirtatiously, her dress tail dragging behind, with a long slit intended to reach her thigh. She pretended, while walking across the stage, to pull her shawl around her shoulder, in an act of reserve, covering her bosom which refused to be hidden. The audience got up again, repeating the clapping and the halleluiahs, each one of them trying to prove to her that he would be the most ardent lover ever. Slowly the auditorium got darker and darker, dimming everywhere except her spot, where it was illuminated. All eyes and ears were fixed, focusing on the circle of her spotlight. Jasim was helped to see her better by being in the front row of the tables, with the best view possible, observing every detail more than anyone else. This did not prevent him from huffing and puffing, sitting in his chair, looking as if he had come running from faraway. Up and down her body, his eyes rose and fell, remembering in detail what his mate Salman had said in describing her fully, and whom he would betray, if given the chance, at any minute. Lully began to sing, showing that she could dance simultaneously as she sang. The whole audience was raving in uproarious excitement. Froth could be seen on some of the drinkers' mouths. The din would have continued without hindrance, if not for one of them getting up, all of a sudden, to smack another who had annoyed him personally. His hostility and emotion quenched with the help of some sitting nearby, the halleluiahs and 'Allah Akbar's, were heard to increase, added to the sighs, damnation and condemnation throughout the auditorium.

There was nobody who was not involved in this performance. Some tried to invoke God to save them. Silence only fell on the surroundings when the gloom and distress was reaching it utmost. Jasim was slighted many times, as Lully was far away from him, busy singing to the others behind him. The darkness in the auditorium decreased gradually; the feeling among the audience became apparent that the singing and dancing would be finished soon. The whole crowd sitting on the chairs roared tumultuously at the end. They expressed their farewell in frustration, clapping their hands and stamping their feet. Lully threw to the audience a lot of hot kisses in the air, acknowledging the awakened desires in their eyes and heads. Salman freely grabbed one of the flying kisses, jumping like a clown, and Jasim did the same. On stage she continued to distribute her precious philanthropy, throwing various signals to the people far away from her or close by. Kisses pouring from her mouth, flying rapidly on smiles launched with her hands. No-one was forgotten. Jasim and Salman were both full of regret when she disappeared once more and the curtains returned to their position, closing their lips in silence. Light spread around brightly in the whole auditorium, showing their hopes to be false.

Sipping from his glass, Salman answered Jasim's further questions:

"Will she come back again?"

"Before the end, for the finale." Salman reassured him.

Suddenly while they were talking, somebody challenged somebody else for the fun of it, calling on everyone loudly to sing a song. They all began together repeating a sarcastic song, well-known to them, about a certain pimp in Baghdad called Dawood, who had no-one to lament him except Fatuma, the prostitute. It lurked always in their drunken memory, from similar Baghdad nightclubs. Roaring together with delight, at the end of a boisterous night, in their hoarse voices:

"Dawood, the lamp lighter with his art died,
Tearing her dress off, is Fatuma."

The crowd roared and whooped in delight, singing hilariously; alcohol and cigarettes were bought in plenty when they finished. A drinker at the other end took off his shoes, the smell of his socks reeking all over the place. Jasim, in his intense hunger, could not help but start eating pickles from the tapas on the table. The audience grew old from waiting, paying rapt attention all the time to the stage curtains. In a sudden frenzy two girls emerged, dancing and singing a silly song, gesturing with their arms stretched out like rifles to make sense of its meaning. The curtains drew back again before a European male dancer appeared quickly, with all the indications showing he enjoyed the most perfect of health. He started tap dancing, reaching up into the air as far as he could, sketching out the corners with his glittering black shoes. The audience regained their comfort when he finished his act and they returned to their normal state of waiting. Snoring was heard coming loudly from one sleeper on a chair, before the presenter came out on the stage, announcing Lully's next number by name. Panic-stricken, he opened his eyes suddenly, and started up from sleep quickly, in case he might miss something. It was enough for him to see that Lully was walking onto the stage, to compensate for his lovely lost sleep and dreams. Lully had obviously changed her dress for another, a red colour now, the colour of blood-red hot pepper. It inflamed the audience, who called to each other to enjoy its taste and heat. Some start to shout excitedly, determined to insist on which of her songs they fancied hearing. She was obliged to do as they wanted, some of them daring to raise their voices in harmony with the requested tune. Her feather-flounced hem started dancing madly, while the glasses on the table were not spared from clashing and breaking. Jasim copied what Salman did, hugging the stage in fright, preparing his lap in case Lully tripped and fell into his lap like thunder and lightening. But all ended peacefully; she was smiling, bowing her tired figure happily. Many kisses were sent into the uproarious atmosphere. Her symbol-laden art was sending signals again to the various individuals and the group. They all stood up to applaud her as the curtains drew together on the stage, finally concealing both the secret of life as well as overt and hidden feelings.

* * * * *

In front of the door of the nightclub Salman said, stroking an American Chevrolet car wistfully:

"This belongs to Lully's escort."

Suddenly, Jasim hit a stumbling block. He finally understood that Lully was not free, she had a man whom she belonged to and he did not want anyone to share her with him. They meekly got on the first waiting bus they saw, crestfallen and slow-witted, surrendering to be taken away to where they belonged, to retreat into the darkness of the sleeping city.

Chapter Three

It was unusual for Sadea to wear her new *aba* when going to clean the dormitory at the end of the summer holidays. She got it out from the wooden chest where it was always kept. The air was full of the Yemeni frankincense with which the *aba* was perfumed. Between her two hands its black material slid softly, reminding her again why she valued it so much. She remembered very well how expensive it had been when she bought it, after much hesitation, from River Street. The shop owner, before she made up her mind, swore to her repeatedly that she would be the one and only winner in the deal. Since then she had adopted the habit of perfuming its folds with essences which she purchased from an Indian in the al-Kadhim district. With love and care she would wrap the *aba* afterwards in a blue and saffron yellow patterned satin bundle. Today was different. She finished putting on her delicate, embroidered dress, putting up her headscarf with artful skill, and headed in a hurry towards the door to leave the house. Her niece Zahra followed her, wanting to go out into the street to play with other neighbour's small children. Sadea rebuked her, unusually, telling her to stay home and be a good girl, leaving quickly and shutting the door behind her.

She carried on walking till she reached the first bus, then took the second, eventually disembarking from the two buses which took her straight to the dormitory, her destination. The feeling of release from the hell of an Iraqi summer made the old deep green eucalyptus trees that lined the street inspire peacefulness and possible rising hope, promising a life worth living. Sadea's slippers clattered beneath the shadow of the trees and the fringes of her damask *aba* danced jauntily. In normal circumstances, she would expect to see Jasim as she had left him nearly two months ago and take the keys from him without much thought or hesitation. She usually found him as before, without noticing any change, as though he was a sheet of paper or a piece of furniture she had left a while ago, and now found again.

As usual she automatically knocked on the door, once or twice or more. Today there was no reply. She tried pressing the bell on the outside door, repeatedly, with increasing pressure and urgency. Her enthusiasm made her listen carefully. At last she was successful. Jasim finally appeared on the steps, coming towards the front gate. Upon seeing her, his eyes glittered as he handed her the keys of the dormitory, telling her that if she needed any help he would be at her service, smiling as he made his kind offer. He noticed for the first time that she also had nice eyes.

Thanking him, Sadea entered the front garden, flicking the hem of her *aba*, deliberately graceful, her hands clinking with the keys dangling like fingers. She opened the wooden front door of the main building, stirring up the dusty air still hanging there. Looking for a clean place, without wasting much time she found an isolated shelf to place her *aba* on. She start opening the abandoned rooms, including Miss Mary's, who before leaving had examined its contents, fearful of dust and damage, and covered its woollen, flesh-coloured seats with brown sheets like tents. This done, Miss Mary did likewise with the exposed portrait photographs of her husband Annis, her nephew Hakmat and her Auntie Najiba, protecting them from the elements by draping remnants of cloth over them. Everything was cleared away for Sadea to start work. All that was left for her was to take off her slippers and her headscarf and declare war on the motionless grime.

She began with the first floor, mainly full of empty beds, forcing her to go carefully in between them to clean, wiping the dust off the windows sills and shaking the bedding on the mattresses one by one and sweeping away all the dirt in her path. Her attention was attracted, while she was in the girl's rooms, by a powder compact, a bottle of nail polish and a lot of pins thrown away heedlessly. Sadea put them aside, away from the dust, with care. Going back to her task, she collected up rags with papers, broken combs, etc. before everything was swept towards the stairs, with the broom climbing down step by step, descending with it all. The ground floor hall greeted her without ceremony. Sadea bustled around, coming and going, dealing with its filth and dirt enthusiastically and getting nearer to the front entrance, the official position of Jasim and his small flowery-cushioned chair. She brushed the dust off the two armrests, shaking the deflated cushion with devotion. The empty place looked as if it was inviting its owner, calling him to sit on it. Sadea felt the same, longing very much to see the chair occupied by him. She swept underneath it, seeing his legs within the space, even hearing the clicking of his worry-beads while he was sitting comfortably. She went round the kitchen, to the shelves and their contents, to the bathroom, with the hand basins. She kept one frayed old toothbrush which she found on the edge of the wash basin to use herself. Time was pressing on; almost galloping, as she cleaned everything around her except herself, without feeling any pangs of hunger although it was four o'clock in the afternoon.

She was hanging her hair under the shower, massaging it, washing her face and neck, gurgling, standing in the bathroom, when she heard Jasim's footsteps approaching. She ran to the nearest room to hide, sheltering in Miss Mary's room, soaking wet, as she recognised his gait very well coming towards her. Without locking the door behind her, she left it ajar in her haste, as she looked for her headscarf and other discarded clothes. The door opened slowly. Her body started to tremble and the silence shattered in the whole dormitory. He did not ask her if she had finished her work, or clear his throat as was his habit to announce himself. She felt the door being shut in a whisper, and an ice cream tub being put on the side and her right hand being lifted gently, making her body fall on the bed all of a sudden, instinctively.

Sadea could have called out for her brother Abood, the policeman Hasan, or anyone at all to rush to assist her. She failed to ask for any help. She was like a ripe date fruit waiting to be picked. Sadea was practising what came naturally to her as a woman. What happened was inevitable when two people, for whom sex was prohibited, found themselves alone together. Now that it was over Sadea opened her eyes, and what did she see? She found an ice cream tub like a pink inkpot, melting slowly on the side table, while on the wall the faces of Annis, Hakmat and Auntie Najiba, full of shyness, were covered with three burkas. No trace of Jasim in the room at all.

*****

No two people would disagree, on seeing Sadea, that she had no particular mark of beauty or ugliness worth mentioning. She was an ordinary woman in every sense of the word. Past thirty-five, exhaustion had played its part in exaggerating her ruined facial features, dragging down her forehead and her brown baggy cheeks. Despite her ability to control her emotions by avoiding temptation, looking at things in the strict manner of 'allowed' and 'not allowed' in the terms of her tradition, she was unable to avoid Jasim. One way or another she used to see him as a saviour. He was capable of making her tiredness in the dormitory into an amusement, satisfying the energy of her hidden desires which nobody else gave a damn for.

She was only fourteen years old when her mother sent her to buy a fish, giving her two *dirhams*. Arriving at the fishmonger's, she found a tall, broad, hairy-chested man, weathered by all the element of the river Tigris and expert in how to gather fish in his complicated net. He soon discovered she could well have been one of those prey. Next to him was a small mound of silver fish scales, removed from the skin of the fish by a knife resembling dagger. As he sat on a woven straw mat, Sadea approached, new to everything, including the wearing of the *aba* and how to put on the veil. She was awkardly holding the black material of the *aba* tightly in place encircling her face. She sat down next to him, close to the squatting women who were sitting there, tossing and checking the fish, selecting what they wanted from the whole pile. Before long the *aba* fell from her head to her shoulder, while she was trying to follow their example. Immediately the fishmonger realised it was his duty to re-fix her *aba* on her head again, laughing cheerfully to reassure her. In no time, he volunteered to choose a beautiful fresh fish for her, promising her in a low, thick voice that it was free if she agreed to become a regular customer. The importance of paying for everything never occurred to Sadea, then; she imagined the fishmonger was a kind-hearted man who sacrificed much for others. She agreed to the deal, finding it easy. She returned to her house after a while, hiding under her *aba* the fish which had been given freely to her. When she arrived home, her brother Abood was there. She showed her mother and brother the fish proudly, pleased that she got it free as a gift from heaven, and never paid the two *dirhams* it should have cost. With hindsight, she was not happy about it now. She explained in detail to them what the tall man wanted from her when he talked to her in a very low voice, offering to keep the fish for her if she became a regular customer. Her mother was in a frenzy, blazing like the hearth. Abood attacked her, snatching the fish, throwing it on the floor and stamping on its backbone with his two heavy shoes. The intestines of the fish burst out from its rear. Her eyes bulged as Abood swore that he was determined to slaughter Sadea as well, right now. At that precise moment, as she ran to her bedroom crying, it occurred to Sadea that the fishmonger was the culprit for ruining the beautiful body of the fish and she too was to be blamed for accepting his dubious offer.

From then on and ever since, Sadea managed to learn how to wear the *aba* with diligence, hiding beneath its cover, like a walking black coal sack with its edges sewn up. She also learned to fear men and their sudden generosity. The atmosphere between her and Abood became calmer, especially after she got the job in the girl's dormitory, believing that security would prevail there. Besides, she had reached an age to be trusted. All of a sudden, without any warning, Sadea became aware of Jasim as a man among the girls of the dormitory. She started to remember she was a woman and the other was of a different sex, not only unlike her own, but different from her brother as well. She forgot the beautiful silver fish which had been thrown beneath Abood's heavy shoes, and to forget the fear of the old things, which never stayed the same as she remembered.

Her increased interest in the girls' overheard conversations began to stir up her feelings. Their comments about sex, male colleagues and girls' amours, awakened her. She would listen to what was said, and how things were going on, and shared their excitement. Her involvement in their activities helped to lessen Abood threats and improved Jasim's image. Their laughter and their jokes during the chit-chat which she shared, mingled agitation with some kind of happiness she had never felt before in her whole life. Sadea started to pick up lipsticks, when she found herself alone in their rooms, or to examine some make up left on the tables when nobody was there. She kept turning it over and checking its contents in inquisitive admiration. She had never been interested in it before or cared about it in her life, till now. At times, seeing perfume bottles on the girls' tables, she would pick them up and be tempted to try some drops in her hands, or spread it over her body with relish, the fragrance on her clothes steadily increasing the flowery wishes within her heart. After all, the hope was there, thinking that Jasim was going to do the decent thing one day. He was going to do what Mullah Hamadi did before, when he asked for her hand officially from her brother, the way they do. Her brother Abood would accept his proposal, especially when he told him that he was a caretaker in a girls' dormitory, had a furnished room and the Ministry of Education gave him twenty dinars each month. She thought she was very near to being rescued one way or the other. The balance of power between her and her sister-in-law, who was always grumbling about her being under her feet in the house, would be improved greatly. She would forgive her malicious past talk and the ridicule. Since the ill-fated incident of the fish, Sadea had started to think about her own future and interest, remembering that the many holidays were years taken from her own.

During all that time Sadea made efforts to gain Jasim's love, slowly. She treated him with fairness and honesty to buy her happiness at a reasonable, negotiated price, paying it without losing too much of herself. She thought that Jasim needed her as much as she needed him. She never thought she was going, one day, to declare war on him, force him by threats while lamenting her miserable fate. Now everything had changed. She rearranged Miss Mary's bed after they had slept together on it, getting up, preferring to leave the dormitory quickly and completely, leaving it clean.

*****

Her anxiety increased when Sadea was asleep at night. Sometimes, she made as if to get up, sitting upright in her bed, protesting in a loud voice. The creaking bed beneath her worried her, expecting it would wake Abood, as he slept near her on the roof terrace. He would find out what had happened to her and stamp on the fish with his shoes. She was always trembling, frightened of his retribution. The days passed by until the end of August, shrouded in dreadful silence. Her daring and joy were dashed, vanished. Instead, her old, bad reputation came back to haunt her. The one who used to be guilty because of the tall fishmonger, one day became guilty again in the face of God and the people. Waking up in the morning she would look into Abood's face and wonder if he had seen or heard something? When would the slaughter be, and how long was she going to live? When Abood went out or returned to the house she was in agony. Panicking about his movements, she would be eavesdropping all the time, waiting for his reaction when he returned home, observing his sayings and actions with the utmost caution. She would wonder whether anyone among his friends or people in the café had told him, after a row, what had happened in Miss Mary's room during the holidays.

It still haunted her how her uncle had started his story one day. He had come to them last winter, sitting around the fire telling them in his rustic accent a story of how his friend Elwan killed his daughter when somebody casually told him in the guest house that 'his *aba* was dirty'. This sentence was enough to make him extremely anxious about the honour of his daughter or sister, as it is well known to mean the disgrace of a female in the family. It was a signal for him to hurry back to his house, intending to get rid of her for good, so nobody could say his *aba* was dirty. That night, when her uncle was sitting telling them the story, Sadea never thought that it would be significant to her one day, let alone apply to her. She was enjoying the conversation, not finding any harm in it, and unconcerned about her brother Abood when he compared what had happened to Elwan with what might also happen to him. His five-year-old daughter Zahra was dipping her bread into her milky tea, while he explained that despite all his love for her, he would kill her like Elwan's daughter if he heard somebody staining his reputation because of her. In his opinion, nobody should blame Elwan for his action. Zahra was looking at her father with admiration and love while he was talking about her, hugging him around the neck after she had finished her tea. That day Abood never mentioned Sadea, as she was so far from suspicion due to her old age. However, the uncle corrected his story, mentioning at the end with regret that Elwan actually overdid it, and rushed into action as his fury took over. It would have been better if he had waited a little; some blamed him afterwards, saying that his daughter was innocent. Abood retaliated with twisted logic departing from the real subject, reminding the audience just in case they did not know:

"In the villages of the South, somebody would say to the man in question that his *aba* was inside out, not just dirty, when it happened that a woman in his house had a bad reputation."

All of those listening agreed, then continued talking about other things, as though what had been discussed a few minutes before had nothing to do with them.

The word Honour, then, obscurely, was always floating around in their house like a balloon full of air. They were so careful not to touch and burst it with a sharp pin, in case it exploded into bubbles. Especially as they all knew that this concept of honour belonged to Abood alone. The women in the house were not interested in examining it, nor cared about it much. They left it on the shelf with its arrogance. Now it came alive, like a stern, long, greedy face wanting to put Sadea on trial. Her punishment was kept on file, registered without any clemency or chance to have her say.

From now on, Sadea tried not to cross Abood's path, avoiding confronting him, in case he remembered something or she would remind him of some act. Her talk of going to the dormitory dwindled, and she never mentioned Miss Mary's return from Lebanon, avoiding the subject of the dormitory altogether. In the meantime, she wished she was employed in the houses of rich people, looking after their children, earning her living through such employment. Albeit she was unable to do that, as Abood usually interfered with her decision, refusing to see her working as a maid in other people's homes. Her work with the government, as he saw it, protected his dignity and respect. Those two concepts, Dignity and Respect, never left his mind; he lived for them, always bringing them up in his conversation.

With Abood and his wife in their bedroom there, Sadea's suspicion stirred and increased. The silence between them made her believe they were discussing how to treat her. As she imagined both were whispering about her fate Sadea behaved in a strained and worried way when she faced her sister-in-law, as if she was pleading for mercy. After a week, Abood said without looking at her:

"When do the holidays end?"

She was startled, as they were eating their breakfast. He repeated the question again; she answered concisely:

"In two days."

She could not manage to express her regret for the end of the holiday, as she normally did. It was a well-known fact, in past years, that Sadea would feel sorry every time the summer holidays finished, but this year was not like any other.

* * * * *

Finally she could not help it. The matter could not be delayed, or be avoided. It was absolutely necessary that she must go to the dormitory in the end. She found the front entrance empty so she quickly darted inside the building. Traces here and there showing that the girls had arrived were in evidence. Some of them came early, as they want to prepare themselves to re-sit the examinations in failed subjects from the previous term. She heard their voices in the halls and was convinced that Miss Mary must also be in her room now. She headed off to see her. The Governess was eating breakfast, the layers of her doughy body settling as she sat, earnestly chewing and biting. After a short greeting to Sadea inquiring about her well being, Miss Mary pulled out from the wardrobe a small bundle, showing her a present she had brought her from Lebanon. It was a copper bracelet studded with imitation rubies made there. At the same time, she told Sadea about Jasim's present, which was a pair of sandals. Unfortunately, they were too big for him, as when she was in Lebanon she thought Jasim's feet were size ten. Quickly Miss Mary closed the subject of presents and moved on to the names of the nine girls in the dormitory who had arrived nearly three days ago. She didn't let Sadea out of her sight and her room until she had urged her to take special care in preparing the dormitory for the coming term. At the same time she handed her the empty breakfast tray which she just finished to take away with her to the kitchen, not forgetting to add also to put the milk and the butter back in the fridge. Her conversation ended with praise for Sadea's efforts in cleaning the dormitory while she was away for the holidays. She was certain that without Sadea the place would not be as comfortable as she found it when she came back from Lebanon.

All the girls were crowded into the kitchen when she went there, several pots of tea and coffee on the table. Some had already finished their breakfast and dressed to go out while others were still in their dressing gowns. Her familiar modest voice greeted them quietly, and one of the girls who saw her first replied with a friendly, sympathetic shout. They made way for her to pass through them. They wanted to pour tea for her, eagerly asking her to join them. Siham insists on Sadea sitting on an empty chair she dragged up for her. What was wrong with starting the day in ease and comfort?

Sadea, trying to make the atmosphere as normal as she could, brought her special cup into the kitchen, worried that the girls might get upset if she refused their invitation:

"Do you like sugar, Sadea? How many spoonfuls do you take in your tea?" one girl asked her.

"As it comes."

The girl was surprised at Sadea's answer, and commented pleasantly with a smile:

"Sadea, you're going to be drinking it!"

"One spoon."

Another girl tapped on the table, suddenly announcing a juicy piece of gossip, heard during her holiday:

"Guess what?"

"What?"

"Wafa is engaged."

"Who's the fiancé?"

"A doctor who graduated in Germany."

"And what about Tarik?"

"She forgot him."

"That quickly?"

"She doesn't love him."

"Why did she encourage him then?"

"She used him, he summarised all the lectures for her. He wrote all the essays, researching in the library all the time."

"This ability I really admire: I mean, to use men."

"They use us; besides, this one didn't own a car."

The giggling increased between them, the gossip and hearsay. They kept talking amongst themselves, discussing their own affairs to the point of forgetting Sadea's existence. Taking full advantage of the situation, Sadea sneaked out without them noticing, while the talk was still going on. She left the kitchen altogether, carrying the mop and bucket, while many different voices mingled intensely in conversation:

"I'm a jealous person."

"Engineers bore me so much."

"What about a pharmacist?"

"A pharmacist is just a merchant."

"Imagine, during the holidays an Arab merchant came to ask my hand in marriage! He owns a private jet."

"And did you accept him?"

"No, no, I don't know him, he proposed through his family and mine. I don't like arranged proposals."

"Perhaps he'll marry somebody else as well after a while, and maybe more than one wife during your life with him."

All of them started to laugh loudly. One girl, who was busy taking out from the oven a hot cake which she had just baked, commented:

"More than two hundred years ago women were burnt, on the pretext of being witches."

"That was in the middle-ages."

"And before Islam, female infants were buried alive."

"Men have no shame."

"I'm going to the shops to buy some new shoes."

"Shoes made in Baghdad are no good. My Auntie brought me a pair of English shoes. Oh my goodness! how beautiful."

"Lebanese shoes are better."

"Only their style is nice."

"The good ones are expensive."

Between them they kept talking, more non-stop chat quite disjointed at times, as conversations went on in twos or threes or all together. Sadea continued going back and forth to the kitchen carrying the bucket, emptying the dirty water and filling it up again. No-one in the whole gathering mentioned

Jasim, or how he had overstepped the mark. Sadea was compelled to go and mop the floor of the corridors and front entrance and found his chair was empty. Stifling her deep desire to ask about him, busy distracted with the thoughts of the day, she was back with him in the room.

* * * * *

It was one o'clock when his figure appeared in the empty kitchen; he was holding up Miss Mary's tray, trying to shield his face with it. Sadea could not look him in the eye, just as he did not try to greet her as before. Ending his problem with her in his harsh voice, he told her simply:

"I ate in the restaurant."

He quickly left the kitchen without waiting for her reply. She realized sadly how she had been waiting for him all this time. She lit the gas stove to prepare Miss Mary's coffee as usual, letting a trembling tear fall from her eye into the blazing flame.

That day Sadea was aware of how Jasim steered clear of her completely. She saw not a single trace of him in the whole dormitory afterwards. He found excuses to stay away, pretending that the dormitory did not need him while the girls were few in number as they had not all come back yet. One week he stayed secluded in his room, slyly avoiding her, loitering between the laundry man Salman and Master Rajab, trying to make things seem ordinary and lessen his burden. Surprisingly, Sadea was seen crying one day. She claimed that her niece Zahra was ill and the doctor said there was no hope of her recovery. Some of the girls' faces showed pity for her and then they busied themselves with their own affairs and talk.

* * * * *

New student faces arrived at the dormitory. The place was filled with their voices. The staircase became noisy with their ascending and descending shoes tapping away. Some of them dumped their empty reed baskets in the kitchen or opened cartons full of food, brought with them from home. Dates and date syrup, pastries which some mothers had tried their best to bake in artistic designs, while others made wonderful Mosul *kubba*. Some notoriously well-known girls were missing; they had not come back this year, as they had finished their studies altogether. Newcomers arrived, excited at the prospect of what would happen to them later, or what they would encounter. Salwa's short hair had grown longer during the holidays, Mayada had put on weight. At the same time it became known that Samea's engagement had been postponed indefinitely, arousing suspicion over the ambiguous reason. Miss Mary hung a notice on the board at the entrance to the dormitory, stating her official administrative instructions. She was emphasizing clearly, as she did at the beginning of every year, the importance of keeping the reputation of the dormitory at a morally high standard and indicating how to prevent it slipping from its lofty values and idealism. When in a good mood, she would talk with the girls, about Jeatta cave in Lebanon and how wonderful the resort of Zahla was, telling them how she travelled to these two places by car and what a surprise it was when, during the journey, she met an old colleague of her husband Annis. This man she met used to work in the post office with him. She added to the listener how he admired her husband, heaping unimaginable praises on him. Wicked girls laughed behind her back, imitating her walk, setting a trap for her, ridiculing the house slippers that she wore, proudly brought back from Lebanon, with their pointed tip like a vase with a feather in it. Wahida did not come back with the others; it was said that she had left college altogether, to marry her cousin Hamed.

Miss Mary expressed sorrow at the news, adding with regret that 'she is a clever girl, so why did she not finish her studies?'

A new girl was seen attached to a colleague of hers and it was said she was in love with him. There was hubbub in one room in the middle of the night, when it was said that Safia was afflicted with hysteria. The girls became acquainted with the college corridors, its laboratories and professors and which students were intelligent and which ones were shallow.

Rumours spread among the girls that Professor Hamdan had failed in his subject and had bought his degree from his teacher. Some agreed or disagreed amongst themselves on how one could buy a qualification. Others reaffirmed that what was suspected was true, as this Professor Hamdan had obtained his degree in America and there are ways you could buy it in such a country. Huda protested, interjecting in the conversation, saying that her brother studied there and gained his degree through nothing but his own hard work. Meanwhile, she ridiculed the degrees obtained from Communist countries. The discussion and argument became heated until suddenly a voice of reason burst into the middle, ending the whole subject. She gave them her cool composed opinion:

"Come on, what's the problem? I see Ph.D. degrees becoming just like the turbaned heads of religious people among us. Everyone who wears one will have to be called 'your Honour'. It is really just for the pride and pomposity of it."

"But it is intimidating."

"Intimidate the ignorant. I wish they would bestow Ph.D.s in the university for subjects like truthfulness, honesty, bravery and mercy."

All of them stared, transfixed, as though they had birds sitting on their heads. Their conversation ended with many different issues not related to the first one at all.

Najla received a letter from an unknown admirer, threatening suicide if she did not reciprocate his love, though he was too timid to put his name at the end of his note. Fighting and jealousy broke out between the girls, secrets were revealed or exposed, a lot of cruel comments and rumours circulated, judgements were passed on innocent people and many relationships were broken up. Not a single finger was ever pointed at the one sitting on the doorstep – Jasim – while Sadea's faults were still there, and well-founded.

* * * * *

Dark winter clouds gathered and passed slowly. On the dormitory floor hemp rope mats were laid. Nine Aladdin oil heaters were brought in to warm the place up. Girls crowded around them, huddling together when they felt cold, as though they were whispering to each other. Sadea warmed herself by getting nearer to the oven in the kitchen, while Jasim was helped by being a friend of Salman's, the laundry man, whose workroom was heated by the steam from the iron. Sometimes he was warm, at other times freezing. Salman's eyebrows became animated as he went on and on about the delicious subject. It was full of forbidden phrases, which Jasim used to be afraid of. Comparing Sadea to Lully became a habit, a sort of medicine to both men. It had a bitter taste to Salman who found a huge difference between the two women:

"Her complexion is grey."

"Don't talk about her appearance, I know it."

"So why on earth did you get involved?"

"You don't look a gift horse in the mouth."

"And she is open-handed."

"She is crazy about me, I swear by Joseph's coat of many colours!"

They go wild with laughter. The clothes being ironed become overheated, and are only cooled down by mentioning the 20th of August when Jasim entered the dormitory with the two tubs of ice cream. Sadea kept pestering him from room to room with her two naked arms outstretched to tempt him. Jasim warned her to stop this naughtiness, to remember the Islamic Sharia and the Prophet's sayings, but she never heeded their prohibitions and commands. She wanted him, persisting in importuning him fearlessly.

"She offered me her cheek today."

"What about her mouth?"

"In the holidays."

"When the craving comes over her."

More loud laughter, while the laundry bottle sprays its saliva. Jasim claps Salman on the shoulder in jest, lest he should be envious. In Sadea, who is generous to Jasim, giving him whatever he wants, Salman sees only decency and chastity, as she is always reserved with others. Still Jasim kept lying, as his falsehoods about his adventures with Sadea grew bigger and bigger. He insisted that he was innocent, assuring Salman he did not want or need her, telling her off, but she was always beside him. Sadea was easy and just like a discarded dog's bone. Jasim would boastfully tell his stories, bragging and imposing his imaginative lies every day on Salman:

"She came to my room to show me her body."

"And what did you think, Sir?"

"Like a dilapidated roof."

The laundry man was not satisfied with this, and continued:

"And what about her secret places?"

"The same, it goes without saying."

In no time, water from the laundry bottle was spraying its saliva on the fabric, hissing with steam again. Salman wisely concluded "She is mad" while his fingers begin to unbutton the shirt, turning it inside out to iron. He enquired:

"Would you want to go with me?"

"Where?"

"To see Lully."

"That Lully is busy."

"And you have enough supplies!"

They winked at each other, knowingly. Jasim suddenly jumped up from his seat, remembering Miss Mary's tray as it was already approaching lunchtime.

*****

Sadea's face became darker, its dullness and gloom increasing day by day. The more Jasim avoided her, the wiser and stronger she became, while he feared to approach her in case she would cling to him in earnest. She, in her turn, shunned contact with him in order not to be vulnerable. Mutual hatred grew between them, loathing each other intensely from a distance with hidden reserves of abhorrence. She also began to flee like a grasshopper from the laundry man Salman when she noticed Jasim's attachment to him. She would avoid passing his shop front as far as she could, full of fear. One day, Salman spoke into the air while she was walking by, flirting with her loudly in a cynical way, trying to claim his share of the booty on offer:

"Ok, my *aba* woman, why are you avoiding me, my darling!"

She turned her face away in the opposite direction while ignoring him. He immediately wanted to humiliate her even more, and taking his revenge in reprisal, he added:

"Miss Holidays!"

Sadea could not bear his many clearly allusive remarks. Salman became part and parcel of Jasim. Why not rib her more with innuendo, teasing her about her stigma and disgrace? He found a ready-made excuse to punish her without any forgiveness, mercy or hesitation. Sadea knew by now for certain that Jasim had not lost any time in letting Salman share their secret, becoming a witness at the scene of her crime. All this time she remained imprisoned in her silence, though he continued his playfulness hand-in-hand with the monotony of the shop. He now found a solution to his boredom by amusing himself in choosing whenever he liked to direct his bow and arrow towards her. Killing time by joking, he quizzed her with one of his mocking remarks, while she was passing his shop in confusion, nearly tripping as she walked:

'What's the use of the *aba* then, my darling?"

Surrounded by sarcasm and irony, her *aba* at that moment made her stumble with embarrassment as it flapped in the wind. Through the open sandals her cold toes poked out rigidly. With all his vulgarity and her burden of guilt, Sadea was powerless to stop him. He started asking her later when and where she would meet him for a date. It was fixed in his mind that she owed him something, which he always reminded her, by his provocative remarks and comments, to pay promptly.

Sadea was unable to stop his attacks or stand her ground, lest he would reveal the secret which had become indisputable to him. She could not tell Jasim about his behaviour. The subject would bring a big lump to her throat and was fraught with pain and danger. Fear and suspicion also reached her from Master Rajab. A glance from the latter was enough to imply menace and anger for the same reasons, filling her with doubt and mistrust. In passing their shops, she was convinced she had become a laughing stock among them, and was continually flustered about how to reach the dormitory. Without mercy or clemency, her scandal was exposed and spread out like dirty clothes on a washing line as she walked by. She did not know what Jasim had said to them, or how guilty he had made her out to be in his stories.

* * * * *

Every evening, Sadea prepared to leave the dormitory with her belongings in a reed basket. That evening the road was deserted except for a few lights in shop windows. She crossed the street in order to catch the first bus that would take her to Bab al-Moadham Square, then the second bus which would be ready and on time to take her to her brother's house in the al-Kadhim district. The crowded bus arrived after a while, with hardly space to stand. Among the passengers, Sadea got on, clinging to her spot, at the same time trying to avoid a big lumpy foot squashed into its shoe, which was rubbing and poking her. Lifting her head after a while towards the owner of the foot, she recognised the face. It was no other than the laundry man, Salman. It was obvious he was following her. He smiled at her when she noticed him. His hand with its gold ring and watch on his wrist were shaking from the movement of the bus. Breathing heavily into her face he asked, demanding and nagging:

"How long will this go on, Sadea?"

The question betrayed his need, blaming her for the delay. He continued:

"Do you want to meet me tonight?"

Covered in embarrassment, she stood awkwardly and her hand clung to her reed basket as though she was hugging her heart. The *aba* whose black fabric enveloped her made her feel like a lioness under its fur. Salman added:

"Forget Jasim, abandon him, enough is enough."

Her hand was burning from clutching the reed basket nervously. The bus slowed down to stop, opening its doors to an empty suburb. Passengers got on and off, while Salman was still busy talking, trying to entice her:

"Or do you prefer the holidays?" He smiled wickedly, laughing out of the side of his mouth, assuring her that he was a witness to what had happened in the room. Sadea turned her face away and the bus slowed down as it approached the next bus stop:

"Until when are you keeping yourself only for Jasim, tell me!?"

She became dumb as a lifeless statue. Many of the passengers heard the last sentence and understood what was going on. The doors opened after a while and Salman jumped off carrying a grudge, full of reproach and hatred with his heavy feet and big head.

She felt safer and after a brave effort, lifted up her face, looking in dread at the people standing around her as though they too were waiting for the verdict. She saw her brother, Abood, among them. The neck of his striped shirt was tight on him, his sharp lips clamped shut like knives ready to cut a rope. Realising that he had heard and seen what happened minutes before, she was without doubt now that he must think there was more than one man in her life, having heard with his own ears the quarrel for and about her. It was impossible for her to repel the waves of anger in his fiery eyes, nor could she calm down the swollen vein in his thick neck. What was said and done in the bus was proof enough for him. Only the details were left for him to fill in, to finish the job completely and tidily. Then he could regain his former peace of mind. The vehicle started to weave right and left like a ship on the high seas defying the eye of a storm, till they both got off near the 'al-A'imma Bridge.' At last reaching their destination, Abood chose to walk in front of her; since reaching adulthood he had always been unwilling to walk with women, anyhow. It was part of the prevailing wisdom of men like him to feel ashamed to talk and walk with women like her. Fearing people's gossip and the notorious suspicion always at the front of their minds. Dust flew up, indicating the imprint of Abood's shoe, marking his stride. He walked on regardless of her, towards their home, entering their dusty street, his teeth biting the air in anger. They felt crowded by each other. After the evening call to prayer, the houses of al-Kadhim were already dozing, crouching on both sides of the road, dark and mute. He preceded her with the vehemence of a bull enraged by wasps, rushing to enter the house. When they got in his daughter Zahra greeted them in her usual manner. She was happy to see them both, after waiting so long for their arrival. Her father Abood asked her a burning question, pushing her aside:

"Where's your mother?"

"In the kitchen."

Her mother emerged from the kitchen, her two hands hanging in the air smelling of cut onions. The aroma of the Anbir rice she was cooking wafted towards them. Surprised, she said when she saw them there:

"Oh, you're back!"

His dryness and the rebuff in his answer showed there was something wrong:

"Prepare yourself to go to your family."

"Why?"

"Your grandfather is dying."

She understood at once that he had died already. Her grandfather had been paralysed for a long time; and all had been expecting the day of reckoning for him.

Sadea entered the kitchen, taking refuge there. She stood close to a barrel of fuel oil, unaware of the danger, while listening to the voices of her sister-in-law and her daughter Zahra. They were getting ready to go out. She recoiled from the thought that both of them were going out and leaving her alone in the house with her brother. The silence became heavy after a while. To fulfil his duty Abood came to her to interrogate her, standing in the kitchen doorway. In his resolve to punish her he took the easiest and simplest path, ridiculing her before questioning her to determine her penalty first herself:

"Are you worth two years' imprisonment?"

She bowed her head, perplexed; what could she say to him now? Would her entreaty help her or would it increase his resolve and determination? She was still standing next to the oil barrel; his imagination took wings. He found what he wanted easily without resorting to a knife. Sadea would do the job for him herself, preparing herself to die without his intervention. He questioned her again just to clear his conscience:

"Do you think it deserves two years in prison?"

He was worried, thinking of what the government would do to him when he killed her, but knowing full well that, as long as the killing was for honour, the usual term of punishment according to Iraqi law was only two years' imprisonment. Standing next to her, he was wondering how lightly he could get away with it. Before long, the idea came to him complete and perfectly clear:

"Do you want a scandal or shall we strike a deal?"

He glanced at the oil barrel with a meaningful look. The oil. The oil. It was the ideal solution to the whole problem. He listened to his Honour again carefully. A scandal about his sister would lead to the ruin of his reputation among his acquaintances and friends. Immediately he came to the point:

"One matchstick will be enough for us," he suggested, drawing out a matchbox easily from his pocket. Looking at her and then at the greenish-grey oily liquid, he relaxed, finding what he was seeking, seeing his salvation, crystal clear:

"Only one matchstick."

He pronounced this with inconceivable sweetness and charm. There was even a smile on his lips when he finished what he wanted to say. He handed her the match as though he was giving her the key to a grand house, to enter and be its owner. The air appeared yellow through her eyes as she took the matchbox, shaking in silence and desperation. Without looking at him, she saw the faces of many men passing through her life, deceiving her. Confident of his plan to get rid of the burden, he left the kitchen. The weight landed on her shoulders, to compensate for her evil act. He promptly decided to leave the house altogether and go out, wanting to leave her alone. In the end, she would decide her own fate. The fate they had agreed upon together needed no trace of fingerprints, nor would any evidence be found.

The matter would be settled by a police sentence in their records and investigations to find the culprit. The whole place was ablaze. The inferno burned everything in its way. Nothing left except old traces of little things here and there. In short, everything new, old, worthless or cherished, whatever was there in the house was destroyed. Abood was relieved that the fire definitively took his sister's life forever. To hell with her life and her wretched fate. What resulted had given him peace of mind. The cause of her death accepted by everyone was fire. It was Fate by divine decree, for sure. The most important thing was that she had vanished forever, completely. The fire consumed the whole kitchen, her bed, Abood and his wife's bedroom, etc. The inferno did not leave any mark or even a reminder of her. Secretly he was relieved by this result; her scandal had disappeared with her without anybody asking what the crime was and what she had actually done. Abood was happy and pleased to assist the police with their investigation into the case. The files of the inquiry were kept on shelves, stuffed with all their certainties. Nobody in the investigation cared to ask if Sadea left the house before or while it was on fire. Their imagination did not lead them to her ashes or remains during the heat of the examination. Nor did anyone ask if she had caused the fire herself for some reason, perhaps. They put aside all possible scenarios about her circumstances, and indulged themselves instead in counting and praising her virtues. They continued habitually to recite the presumed dead person's qualities and merits, which they suddenly discovered after her death. From the day they thought she had gone they started eulogising the memory of her soul, each one lying to the other in such situations while they knew perfectly well it was a lie. What really remained of her were only rumours and whispers among those people who had no relevance to her case. Tales circulated now and again among them; no one was sure of their truth or how much they could be trusted. Some of those people said they saw her – in the town of Basra, or in Kerbala, or Iran, or Kuwait. She was working as a servant. So the rumours said.

(Written in 1968)

Postscript

Such rumours and hearsay lost their importance, especially when war flared up between Iraq and its neighbour Iran in 1980. This war raged on for eight years. It took many young lives and ruined an abundance of both material and human resources. All peace-loving people in both panic-stricken countries were alarmed and saddened. During this time, the nouveau riche class spawned by the war was considered to belong to the ruling party then in power. They alone enjoyed what remained of Iraq's wealth and fortune. Decent values and virtues died and other traits and concepts appeared instead. Behaviour which used to be considered extremely backward was now practised among people who would have been ashamed to be seen acting thus in the past. Unjust treatment was not reserved for females and underdogs, but prevailed widely. Some started a power struggle which gave rise to conflict throughout the country for control of unjustly obtained positions. The atmosphere in Iraq was permeated with suspicion and hatred.

During this time, as a consequence of years of neglect by the cruel self-seeking urban elite, village society came to the fore. It carried a heavy burden of peasant mentality and traditions, feudalism and nepotism, exhausted and worn-out. The village, which had never been valued by the city, for once was given its due. Now the downtrodden village started to rule and control the city itself. It became normal for some people to hide or change their names or surnames, in order not to attract attention, just to keep out of sight of the secret police or the informers who were rife everywhere and to avoid being seen or recognised by the government which swamped the length and breadth of the country with its agents. Such informers, both inside and outside Iraq, started to sell their consciences for money, agreeing to report even on their friends, family and neighbours.

Suddenly, Salman the laundry man became the head of the ruling party office in the whole district. Pictures of the intimidating new president, surrounded by mottos of the ruling party written in thick Kufic script, hung on the wall of his shop instead of sluttish naked women and entertainers. He encouraged Jasim the caretaker to become a party member and join the ruling party, offering him money and various privileges. Jasim did not hesitate to do so. Hence he became eager to attend party meetings and celebrations, enthusiastically clapping and shouting party slogans while listening to the hackneyed poems that glorified the fearsome new president and the party, praising the Arab nation. Meanwhile, he started disparaging the Persian "Magi", (despite the fact that he was not quite sure what the word meant). After a while he was ordered to spy on Miss Mary and the girl students as part of his job. Without objecting or hesitating he obeyed the order instantly. He carried out the task as best he could, with apparent tranquillity and happiness. Although he was overheard to say that he did not enjoy the new job fully, as Miss Mary applied for her retirement, claiming she had reached the working age limit. She went back to her own family hometown in Mosul to live out the rest of her days.

A new governess was appointed in her place. Young, dynamic, full of enthusiasm for the ruling party. She treated the girls and Jasim with the harshest discipline. The hostel's atmosphere turned nasty, fit only for writing accusatory political reports to harm and damage its inhabitants. With eagle eyes the new governess watched each student, measuring them openly against certain criteria full of vindication and malice, taking revenge for a long and deprived past. Her role now was to alert the people in charge, in order to punish others and enjoy the power bestowed on her at that moment.

Just as happened before, when the laundry man Salman suddenly became responsible for the party machine, he now started busying himself to fulfil another ambition. Following the same route, he prepared to become a candidate for membership of the National Council. He was rewarded at once for his previous services to the party, satisfying his ultimate desire. His name was included on the list of candidates for membership of the council and he was selected as an honourable MP in reward for his loyalty.

Again, no more than two years after the war ended with Iran, Iraq suddenly attacked a second neighbour. This time it was Kuwait, on the second of August 1990. There in Kuwait, Iraq did its best to ruin the notion of good will between neighbours by looting and destruction, occupying it for six months. Kuwait spared no effort, verbally or in material terms, to get rid of the invaders at any cost. Help was sought worldwide, from large and small countries, asking for their fleets, planes and all weapons necessary to get rid of the aggressor. As Iraq disobeyed the UN ultimatum to withdraw, it faced a fierce joint assault by thirty countries. It was a horrible, hellish war; a huge calamity adding to the other catastrophe already inflicted on the Iraqi people. This war demolished everything left in Iraq; dignity, pride, and all the infrastructure of its economy and social order. At that moment some of its people revolted against the regime, while others fled abroad as refugees. Soon the uprising was suppressed, due to lack of organisation and disagreement amongst the insurgent masses. Four million went into exile, scattered all over the globe. Some who stayed in Iraq had to face rape, hunger or exposure to corruption and harsher measures of oppression. The frail and young children were left to suffer. Some died for want of medicines and from the spread of disease, especially after the implementation of the sanctions imposed on Iraq in 1991 by the United Nations as punishment for its aggression against its neighbour.

Sadea was forgotten, amidst what was happening in Iraq. What remained of her was on the margins of peoples' minds. A few witnesses, who happened to travel abroad and who had known her well, continued to spread rumours among others. They said that they had seen Sadea in person, sitting on the pavement in Amman City in Jordan, selling cigarettes, dates, beads or combs. Most of these travellers were female students who had met her in the dormitory. They knew her and she knew them well too. They said that in spite of her heavy enveloping *hijab* and her fear of talking to them, nonetheless they recognised her. The police never took any notice or interest in such a subject. They were busy facing horrifying new crimes in the country, produced by the changing economic circumstances and shattered security.

Nobody cared to investigate Sadea's death, especially Abood, who was satisfied with the police conclusion long ago, content with their verdict that she had died as a result of the fire in their house. Like them, he closed the file completely. The issue was relegated to the past; where he considered it buried for ever. However, at the same time he stayed alert, assiduously denying whatever rumours he heard about the cause of his sister Sadea's death, always insisting to his friends and acquaintances that she died because of her Fate written by divine decree. The fire was fuelled by the barrel of oil. At times he added, putting the blame on her, that perhaps the fire itself was caused by her negligence. In the meantime, he became fanatical about religious customs and traditions and ordered his wife and his daughter Zahra to wear the *hijab*. In his turn he prostrated himself every day to read the Koran morning, noon and night. He would exaggerate by declaiming in a high-pitched voice, in order to be heard by his neighbours and anyone passing his door. His enthusiasm in reading

Quranic Sur'as would reach a climax when he came to verses indicating the sins of infidel women, their wickedness and their aberrant ways of disobeying God and husband. He always assumed as he read, smugly, that he was the witness who had never been touched by deception. He also started to attend the five daily prayers in the nearby mosque at the appropriate times. Meanwhile, he was preparing himself to carry out the obligation of the al-Hajj pilgrimage to Mecca, to gain the right to be called "al-Haji", as is the custom. The whole neighbourhood afterwards heard and saw Abood enjoying the title of "al-Haji" on his return.

During all this time, instead of showing fear of God in his behaviour, Abood became more and more concerned to satisfy only other people, always showing ostentatiously that he was fasting, praying, going on the Hajj, fulfilling all the rituals of religion one by one. The result was that instead of taking care to obey God by looking after his creatures with mercy and honesty – as true religion orders its followers to do by not killing, lying, being cruel, hypocritical, treacherous, greedy, mendacious, or spreading gossip – Abood has now neglected all these commandments. He has put them aside entirely. His only concern and priority is to continue making people approve of him. He is now frightened only of other people. People have taken the place, in Abood's behaviour, of God himself.

(Completed in 1997)

Lightning Source UK Ltd.
Milton Keynes UK
173932UK00001B/36/P